DINNER AND DEATH
(A Carolina Pennsbury Mystery)

by

Helen Grochmal

For information, email **Cozy Cat Press**, cozycatpress@aol.com or visit our website at: www.cozycatpress.com

COZY CAT
PRESS

ISBN: 978-1-939816-47-4

Printed in the United States of America
Cover design by Nicole Spence
www.covershotcreations.com

1 2 3 4 5 6 7 8 9 10

Thank you to my friends in the community who encourage my writing, especially Judy, Cele, Mary Ellen and Angelika. You and others here make the world better with your kindness.

CHAPTERS

Permanent Members of the Dining Table

CAROLINA—The schoolmarmish leader of the dinner table who lives by the word of God and the wisdom of the great writers of literature. She has an eye for evil and human puzzles and a cane she knows how to use to protect her friends.

ANNIE—Carolina's best friend, an all-American solid woman who helped win WWII. She often later remembers things she has seen and heard that help Carolina solve mysteries.

MARGIE—The sometimes whacky but intelligent member of the group whose speech meanders under stress. Her calico cat, Apolonia, is accepting and sensitive, the last cat in the world who should be a target for murder.

DOT—A not so wealthy woman who wears different hats as a barometer of her feelings. She has insight and often gives well-intended advice but with an edge she can't help.

RITA—A well-off widow who shops and then discards her things like used prune pits. What she really wants is another husband to travel with although she likes her friends too.

Temporary Seat Members

MIKE—A man who acts like a charming Irishman of the old days but who may be a phony. What is he looking for at the Courte, especially after he has been insulted?

FRIEDA—A woman who says she only enjoys talking to men about men's things. She hates cats, but would she go to great lengths to kill one?

PAULA—A cipher as a person who seems agreeable but depresses everyone. Can she kill by boredom?

CHAPTER 1: THE SIXTH DINER

Carolina Pennsbury sat in a reverie at the dining room table in the old folks home—*that is, Independent Retirement Community,* she corrected herself severely. She didn't want to turn into one of those people who thought one thing and said another, hiding it from their friends. Her rebellious self fought against editing her words if she thought them, but Carolina was not often rebellious. She was a good woman with a benevolent spirit. She would never think anything really hurtful. *Just don't carry on,* Carolina's schoolmarmish voice told herself. *Don't be self-indulgent. Just don't!*

"The thought is father to the deed." Where did that come from? she complained to herself. *Maybe Shakespeare.* She had been thinking about Shakespeare for days now. She did that when she was upset. Times at the dining table were in transition again. The powers that be at the "Independent Retirement Community" had one empty chair at a dining table in her corner of the universe and were about to assign a new diner to her table. No one had any say in this process, except maybe during the first week when the new diner or one of the current diners could if they

were willing to make a federal case out of it with Management and accept the consequences. Of course, the seated group of five, now friends, who ate there would not want to hurt anyone. Rejection could be a severe blow at this time of life, at any time of life really, but adolescence and old age were the worst times for it in Carolina's opinion.

They had achieved a sense of satisfaction with their group, had bonded as real friends, especially after solving the last murder and surviving the evacuation in the time of the flood. This satisfaction was threatened when the Dining Room manager said another person was to be assigned to their little group. No one knew what the wrong addition to the table could bring. Carolina thought of the wrong person in Shakespeare. Iago, the treacherous friend in *Othello*, came to mind.

She thought about Laertes, the brother of Ophelia and son of Polonius, in *Hamlet*. He never went looking for trouble, and then a friend murdered his father and drove his sister to suicide and finally he himself was used in an evil plot by the King. She began to wonder who was the one most wronged in the play. Hamlet lashed out, hurting innocent others, seemingly unrepentant of it, while Laertes' heart seemed true to his family.

She looked up to see four pairs of eyes on her.

"What are you thinking about, Carolina?" asked Annie, her best friend.

"I guess I was wishing for someone really interesting at our table."

"You mean not like us," laughed Margie, the younger woman among them, in her mere 60's. Margie was having a hard time adjusting to the retirement home, her husband having recently divorced her to chase other women—any and all women except her—Margie claimed.

"Be careful what you wish for, you might get it," said Rita, the richest and most stylish of them all, although not the brightest. "We dodged a bullet with that last woman they sent here last week. Remember she found the food inedible and left the dining room crying after two days? That was the last we saw of her. I wonder where she went for good food."

"We should keep in touch in case she finds a place," laughed Margie.

"I wonder who we'll get next," piped in Annie. "Let's bring more stuff down to put around the table and move our chairs so it doesn't look like we have enough room."

"Dining management may be stupid sometimes but they can still count to six," said Margie, referring to the number of places at the table. "The place got more people after that flood, so they insist now on a full complement of diners at every table."

"Some of them are only staying until their houses get fixed," said Carolina.

Margie, the best educated and smartest one after Carolina, said, "Maybe. But hardly anyone escapes from here after they've been sentenced. You know, like in *No Exit*." She got blank looks except from Carolina who looked disapprovingly at her.

"Not that you're like the people in hell," hurriedly stammered Margie, who couldn't stand to offend anyone, but managed to do so with her attempts at apologizing.

"What are you talking about us being people in hell?" grumbled Dot.

"Just a play," said Carolina, trying to change the subject and where Margie was going with her unfortunate conversation. "The people from the flood will leave. They just moved here for a while for the meals and because some of the apartments are furnished with things from the model apartments. They can move out easily."

"What about their leases?" asked Margie.

"I wonder if they had to sign at least a year's lease like us. Management might want some fast money and maybe they'll get a few who will stay," said Carolina.

"You would think there would be at least one gorgeous man in the bunch," said Rita, who was really looking for a man who liked to travel.

"We had our share of gorgeous men before, and you know what happened there," said Dot with sarcasm.

"They can be helpful in the day and fun at night, but I would just as soon have a radio." Margie said this in a nervous sort of way. "Uh," she added, embarrassed at their puzzled glances. "I was watching Zazu Pitts in the old movie *Passion Flower*. She said something like that about men. You know, she acted a lot like Olive Oyl in the comics."

"Practice your imitations before you show them to us," advised Dot.

They got their desserts and were ready to leave in good time before they were shooed away before the second seating guests arrived. This time the table cloth had not been taken out from under them while they were sitting there with their tea.

Margie collected the walkers for Annie and Dot and they left in a line. Annie, an all-American can-do woman in all other areas but walking, was a reigning Queen as she left, nodding to those still seated as she swept her way out with majesty. The group made an early night of it with everyone deciding to go to their own apartment, a few stopping to get their mail and newspapers.

Annie and Carolina got in the middle elevator together, the other elevators being on the far ends of the building.

"This table harmony can't last," said Carolina. "It's all so agreeable and boring."

"You want trouble?"

"Excitement at least," complained a usually uncomplaining Carolina.

"I thought we had enough of that with the murder. Do you want us all to join those raunchy databases like Margie says her husband did? She would have to be hospitalized if we did. I have a feeling her ex wears a different toupee and make-up in his pictures, depending on the subscribers."

"I don't know what I mean. More than this. I can't stand another dreadful new diner. They give us the strange ones, you know, that no other table will have," said Carolina.

"I wonder why," laughed Annie. She looked appropriately superior and warned Carolina of her foolishness. "If we have to choose between love and war with another one, I pick love. But the status quo of an empty seat is better."

"Variety is the spice of life," said Carolina who usually avoided clichés. "Well, maybe we get enough variety with those concoctions they make us eat here. I did think the quiche with bacon served with potato pancakes was bad for our cholesterol myself. I did get excitement of a sort seeing if anyone would have to be taken away from the dining room for artery detox."

"I liked it."

"There's an announcement here for the health fair Saturday," said Carolina as she looked at her memo from Management that she had been given at the concierge desk. "They are having demonstrations on healthy cooking and how to avoid too much saturated fat and sugar. The chef from here is going to give the talk. Look at this flyer. 'Avoid those frozen dinners that are not healthy for you!'"

They both laughed.

Annie released the hold button that was letting them continue their conversation illegally (according to a recent memo from Management) and said good-night to Carolina. Carolina went on up to her floor and made the long walk to her apartment which was near one of the far exits. She didn't know that this was the time to be at her most protective and vigilant of her little flock. She really needed to be watching the behavior of others who entered or who were part of their community. But surprise was usually the element of the attacker.

Little did any of the women know that a mind full of evil and plots almost as bad as anything in Shakespeare had set its sights on one of the women, not caring a bit who got in the way and might have to be disposed of. New people at the Courte were accepted at face value. They came to live with them in the same, sometimes very isolated, spaces. Who knew which new ones would come with hidden murderous intentions? Who knew which familiar faces harbored old grudges?

CHAPTER 2: MIKE LOOMS

The next day, five women carrying more purses than seemed necessary for an army and an extra cane or two filed into the dining room to take ownership of their new table of five. They exuded confidence. Dot wore a hat like a Roman helmet, one almost expected to see a spear in her hand. People stared, standing back as the army marched by. The women sat up straighter than usual, befitting soldiers.

"Where did you get that hat in time, Dot?" asked Carolina.

"This is not my first battle," answered Dot.

Chairs were adjusted to fill the bigger spaces around the table, canes and walkers parked closer to the table than usual, carry-on things and large purses taking up more space at the table or hanging down between the diners. Everything said, "This is ours—our table, our circle, our territory!"

"I think we did it," giggled Margie.

They waited for the server to bring their menus and planned on telling her to take away the extra place setting.

Then a genial man resembling the late actor Pat O'Brien approached their table saying, "And a grand day to you, ladies!" He was clean shaven with an oval-shaped open face. His hair was white with a receding hairline.

"I was told to sit here with you darlin' ladies for our nightly repast."

He stood there a time while the dear ladies took him in. They had been enjoying their dream of a table of five. Now there was another to share their battleship. He looked like he expected to be captain.

He started to clear his throat in impatience while the group picked up their things from the table, found places for them on the windowsills or floor and moved their chairs to make room for Mr. Irish character actor from old black and white movies. He sat down at the place they had made for him with his back to the pillar and no view of the dining room. Sometimes the servers stacked the dirty plates on a makeshift drop table behind this seat. The person sitting with his or her back to it was startled when the dishes crashed behind their heads. This new diner was a little cramped between the table and the pillar with his potbelly. (The ladies were nervous. They might have made his seat too uncomfortable for him. It was tradition for the residents to jockey for the best places whenever there was a change in seating, sometimes with the new person getting the best seat somehow. This diner looked like he might be hard to handle.)

They all looked at their menus and discussed the choices.

"You ladies look a bit down at the heels. Did anything happen lately? Bad news?"

"No," said Carolina. "We just take our food seriously."

"They have corned beef and cabbage about twice a year. Well, at least once on St. Patrick's Day. The cabbage is green." This remark was from Margie who couldn't stand uncomfortable situations.

"And a special day that will be," smiled the new diner. "Call me Mike."

The women introduced themselves by first names after that. Round one went to Mike.

"They aren't writin' this menu in language a plain Irishman can understand. What is 'Scallops Meuniere'?"

"Fried scallops," answered Rita, who was no gourmet but had taken over as the table's culinary advisor from Lillian, a former dining companion who really knew her stuff. Rita had apparently bought and studied some cook books recently.

"I see I'll be gainin' even more weight here," Mike said, patting his substantial belly.

The server came to take their order.

"I'll be havin' what this nice lady will be havin,'" he said, nodding towards Rita when it was time to take his order.

Rita beamed. Carolina thought, *Rita will be the first to cave if she is attracted to this very charming Irishman.*

He looked at Dot. "What a fetchin' hat you're wearing, Mrs.?"

"She's a Miss," said Rita hurriedly. "Like we said, call her Dot. Call me Rita. I'm a widow."

"I'm sorry to be hearin' about your loss. I'm sure your husband was a darlin' man."

"Oh, he was," said Rita. "But life goes on."

Mike looked at Dot and asked, "Is it your tradition or religion that keeps you wearin' a hat?"

"No, I like hats."

"They're her personal barometers," giggled Margie, who seemed uncharacteristically silly tonight to Carolina.

Dot glared at Margie.

"Do you have any green ones?" asked Mike to get over the awkwardness.

"Of course, green is a popular color," Dot answered without a smile. She was not going to be so easily won over.

Dinner progressed slowly, but manners won over disappointment for all of them. Their pleasure in a new guest and a possible friend increased. It was nice to have a man around the dull place. Hopefully, he would have some new stories to tell; they had heard all of their own, several times in fact.

Carolina hoped there would be no rivalry. So far Mike had not indicated a preference for anyone, responding to each who showed friendliness to him. Maybe he would get tired of woman talk and move to a more masculine table. She did notice that Mike's slight brogue lessened as he talked more.

"What part of Ireland are you from, uh Mike?" she asked. She preferred last names except with friends but that was not going to be the way things were going apparently.

He laughed. "I'm from right up the street and over the bridge in New York. There were some fine slums there when I was young. I was a friend of the Archbishop when we were growin' up together. We took many an apple from a truck without payin', back then when we were hungry."

Carolina and Margie exchanged glances. They both remembered an old movie like that but with turkeys not apples.

"Were you here for the fire alarm testing the other day?" said Rita to be polite.

"Oh, the Banshee, I call it. I am glad I heard it before it went off in the middle of the night."

"That's how most of us learn of it," complained Dot.

Toward the end of dinner, one or two women from other tables started to come over to Mike to say hello, "just in passing," although they came to his far corner location from different parts of the room. Mike seemed extremely pleased. His smile and eyes lit up. Margie looked suspicious. She had had experience with that look not long ago.

Beverly, who was about 110 years old but admitted to 94 tottered over in spike heels and highly flipped jet black dyed hair from another era. She asked Mike how long he was here for. She actually batted her false eyelashes.

"As long as you lovely colleens will have me."

His fake Irish accent seemed to take the polish off the man a bit for Beverly. Her dream was still for a nice rich man, preferably a stockbroker from the upper west side, who gave her lots of jewelry like her first husband. She said good-bye and turned around with her shiny tight leather jeans and felt a hand on them. It was a quick but experienced feel. The other diners had seen it. Their jaws dropped.

Dinner was over. They started collecting their walkers and canes and many other props, all thinking: *How do we get rid of him?*

Mike was saying, "And where are you lovely ladies off to? May I join you?"

They looked aghast as they saw he was standing where they had to pass by closely in the aisle.

Margie looked wildly for a way out. She still felt married. She did not want to be manhandled. Carolina knew she herself would say something not very complimentary. She was not about to be sexually harassed at this time of her life. Annie laughed. She thought it might be fun, much to Carolina's censure. Dot thought, "I'll run over his foot with my walker." Rita wondered if he could be rehabilitated. She hated to give up her plans for going dancing with him and to museums.

Their own plans of escape were derailed when Ike came up from behind and pulled Mike aside. "Play poker, do you?"

Ike made every woman's heart beat fast and every man respect him for his brains and masculinity. He was hot although he was in his 90s. Mike sensed he was being given an opportunity to join the "elite."

"I like a good game as long as there's a little whiskey with it."

"We can't drink in the game room but we might have a private game someday if we get a good enough group."

The women made their escape while Ike and Mike talked "man talk."

Carolina whispered, "Maybe Ike can adopt him at his table."

Annie said, "Will gambling win over grabbing women?"

Margie huffed, "Sex will win. I've seen that look before."

"I'm afraid you're right," said Dot.

"I wonder if he likes to travel," mused Rita while her friends looked appalled. "I guess not," she quickly assured them, social pressure being what it is.

The gang got distracted by the other people leaving and chatted with friends, adding their share of the after-dinner gridlock that made the Dining Room manager despair.

The manager gave herself a pat on her back, thinking that Mike would work out well with "the five old duenas who needed a man to pay attention to them."

Carolina's dining group got out of line before the bend in the corridor that would take them to the middle elevator and concierge desk. They formed a circle in the corridor leading to one of the wings. The place consisted of a central part made up of the concierge desk, mail boxes, library, common activities rooms and the middle elevator. The favored apartments on the three other floors were near this elevator. Two wings led away from this part of the building to apartments near exits and elevators of their own. Usually people who could walk well took these farther apartments for privacy.

"How do we get rid of him?" whispered Margie, gathering the women around her.

"It's too soon," said Carolina. "We need to use our veto carefully."

"Smack him," said Dot. "I hate mashers. We have canes and walkers and hands to smack him with if he touches any of us."

"We'll get in trouble for that with Management and maybe the police and especially our children," said Annie.

"He might be a nice man if his needs were met," bravely volunteered Rita. She backed off again. "Uh, I don't mean I'm going to satisfy his needs."

"Should we draw straws to see who will?" asked Annie with laughter in her eyes.

"Excuse me, ladies," said the subject of their conversation, Mike, appearing abruptly, a look of hatred in his eyes and all trace of his Irish accent gone. He scowled at each of them and pushed his way through the middle of the group, storming down the hallway and out the far exit.

They stood in embarrassment.

"I guess that takes care of him as a dining partner," said Carolina.

CHAPTER 3: SOCIAL CONDEMNATION

The table friends met in subdued tones at the next usual dinner time. People looked quizzically at them, many with disapproval. The onlookers' eyes said that it was the women's fault that the nice new guy, Mike, had not come down to dinner that night. Rumors abounded.

Margie mumbled something.

"What was that, Margie?" asked Carolina.

"Harpies! Look at their eyes."

"Now, now," said Carolina. "You're imagining things. Besides, it's the men as well as the women who are looking at us. Harpies were *women* in mythology."

"I wonder what he said to them," said Rita. "People here are usually blasé about seating disputes."

"We'll learn soon enough," said Annie. "What's for dinner?"

"It's wine day," said Rita. "Don't forget to ask for it or we won't get it."

"It's lasagna and cheesecake for me," said the more than plump Margie.

"I don't know. The enchiladas with rice look good. And blueberry pie with ice cream," said Annie.

Carolina shook her head. "You know what happens when you eat Mexican food, Annie. You can't talk for a day."

"Maybe they have a new cook who makes the food milder. I think that Mexican cook left," she replied.

"He may have come back just for you, Annie," laughed Margie.

They ate their lethal food quietly until distracted by some intruders outside their window. Evidently, Mike still had a car. The five ladies looked in dismay as Mike gallantly led Beverly in her high-heeled boots from the parking lot up to the sidewalk in front of their table and large window. The couple looked in from outside and pointed at the women at the table.

"Well, I guess we know who alerted Mike that we were having a mean conversation about him the other day," said Dot.

The whole dining room took in the corner tableau. The five ladies felt that almost everyone was rubbing one index finger over the other at them in the old kid's gesture of "shame."

"Ah, life goes on," said Carolina. "We've been through more than this together."

After dessert, Loretta, a large domineering woman who liked to bully people, came over to their table saying pointedly, "I heard from the concierge that Mike is giving a party next week for everyone to meet him. He's paying a lot of money for it. He ordered a big cake. Will you girls be coming?"

"We don't know," said Rita. "We hadn't heard."

As Loretta left, Annie said loudly as a challenge, "Who would have thought that Beverly liked being goosed?"

"We all did," said Dot.

"Let's wait until everyone leaves. I don't want to run into Mike," said Margie.

"We can't live in shame," said Carolina. "The only thing we did wrong was not talking about him in private. We should have known better."

They left last anyway. It seemed the wait staff didn't like them anymore either and had served them slowly.

"What is this spell that Mike has over people? It's bizarre," complained Dot.

"Ignore it," said Carolina. "It will go away."

"Nobody cared when I was repudiated and rejected from Rolanda's table," grumbled Margie.

They left in a broken line.

"Should we face it out in the lobby?" asked Rita.

"Not unless Floyd is back from Florida." Annie loved to sing songs after dinner with heartthrob Floyd playing the piano. Ike and Floyd were the two men in the "Senior Retirement Community" over whom most women pined even though most couldn't understand why. But, sexual power is sexual power at 19 or 90. Ike was like a pirate with his forceful attitude and Floyd a lounge star in his perfect snakeskin shoes.

"Floyd's not back," said Rita.

The women walked to the lobby to get their newspapers and mail. They left the concierge desk. Some friends said hello. Others didn't. They heard conversations that stopped when they went by. They saw a sign on the end of the desk asking everyone to come to Mike's welcoming party and to be sure to thank Mike for it.

"What's the movie tonight?" asked Annie quickly. Annie went to the movie every night except when she had visitors.

The Luck of the Irish," said Margie. She doubtfully added, "I guess co-incidences do happen."

"I'll go anyway," said Annie. "Who'll come with me?" she asked hopefully.

No one bit. They dispersed for the night.

CHAPTER 4: FRIGID FRIEDA

People assembled for dinner the next day.

"How was your day?" asked Carolina.

"Did you see the poker table when you came down?" asked Dot. "Mike was really getting cozy with the regular poker players."

"He's certainly gregarious," said Carolina who wanted to downplay the recent incidents.

"We have lots of friends too," said Annie defensively.

"Speaking of friends," Margie said tentatively, "I have some I'm not too happy with on the internet."

"Who?" asked Dot.

Suddenly they were interrupted by a frowning face that said, "I was told to sit here."

The stranger plunked her substantial body in the empty chair that had been vacated by Mike.

The women looked at her hopefully and said their introductions and welcomes.

Frieda, after saying her name, got down to why she was there, reading some things from the menu: Ham or Fried Chicken, Curly Fries, Buttered Herb Noodles, and Corn O'Brien.

"You can't go wrong there," said Margie. "Corn O'Brien? I wonder if Mike is spreading his influence to the Chef. Maybe the next menu will be all Irish dishes."

"We can't help you with the daily menu," said Rita, trying to get away from telling the newcomer about their experiences with Mike. "It's pretty much of a disaster with salt and cholesterol. I would recommend the baked chicken patty, uhm, breast, from the basic menu with salad and green beans. It's really just a frozen patty."

"Is that what you're getting?" asked Frieda.

"Well, not exactly," admitted Rita.

"It doesn't matter," Frieda said, "Salt and that stuff doesn't bother me. I have a great metabolism. We all do in our family." Everyone stared at her ample frame bursting out of its coverings. Margie, who was overweight too, but knew her failings only too well, giggled and coughed.

After ordering and the soup being served, Carolina went back to the subject of Margie's disappointments on the internet.

"I bought a lot of personal teapots, you know," said Margie, "'tea for one' things. I keep getting them. One day I got three of them from different people and can't use any of them. They never said anything special about defects and such, and you're supposed to tell people about that if you don't see it in the pictures online. Well, one pot wobbles on the table. I tried all sorts of tables, and it still wobbles. Another seller said 'single cup' pot but I could hardly put a half cup of water in it. And the third came saying, 'For Display Use Only' on the bottom. I can't use any of them for our tea parties. I didn't give the sellers top ratings. Then I got a terrible message from one of the sellers calling me names like *coward* and such. I got a letter in the mail from another of them with some tea bags in the envelope saying to put them in a cup and add hot water to them or something like that. I wrote him a thank you letter back for the teabags but then reread his letter and thought it was sarcastic. The two who contacted me asked me to reconsider my rating and upgrade them. I would have before, but now I can't in conscience do that. I don't want anyone else treated like I was. Any substance could have been in that letter. I didn't hear from the third person but I might have given him or her a 100% rating to avoid trouble. I don't open my online messages anymore on the site so I don't know what they said after that."

Annie said, "I don't use the internet. Not too many of the people here my age do. My children get me everything I need. I don't need much."

"I get things online sometimes like lingerie," said Rita. "But I like to go to New York to places like Tiffany's for jewelry. Stones can be substituted, you know, unless you buy from reputable establishments. The things I get and don't like, I give to my son to return. (*More like leave them in the trash room*, thought Carolina. Carolina had a hard time getting expensive things back to Rita, often checking the trash room at night when Rita was in one of her buying and discarding moods. Rita was a bit superficial but looked great since she had lots of money and knew how to spend it. She spent most of her time buying expensive things she didn't really care about and disposing of them in the most convenient way for her.)

"I love hats," said Dot, who wore different ones all of the time. She spent most of her discretionary money on hats. She was wearing one of her middle of the road cloche ones now, in red. "Especially vintage hats," she continued. "A little wear shows its history. I hate the new ones that masquerade as vintage on the databases. They're just cheap folding hats made to look vintage in the pictures. I just don't bother to review them when they disappoint me."

Frieda said, "I think you should always give good reviews. You don't know how much these people depend on money in this age. My son got laid off and had to move away. He can't take me with him where he lives. He travels now. His wife left him."

Margie defended herself. "I wouldn't have given them poor reviews, and the products were not even that bad, if they hadn't abused me. Some of the sellers do beg buyers not to give them bad reviews. Apparently they're encouraged to get stars for getting 100% great reviews. Sellers brag about it online and some sellers berate anyone on their sites who would give them less than a 100% rating. Some say to contact them online before giving any criticism, but I didn't know how to do it then. I only found out when they began to yell at me. A lot of us buyers don't understand the computer sites perfectly at first. And the overseeing site itself says to be honest in reviews."

"I buy things too on the internet since I don't drive anymore," said Carolina, obliquely referring to her fading eyesight that she tried to keep hidden from friends for their sakes. Carolina took care of other people but felt uncomfortable in the receiving mode. "I never ran into your problems, Margie."

"I never did either until I started to buy teapots. My advice is don't ever buy used little teapots online. They come with a curse."

"How is Apolonia?" Carolina asked, thinking the teapot topic had been exhausted. Margie's cat had had an episode of apparently seeing something invisible in Margie's old apartment. The little creature constantly lived in hiding or was forever trying to get out the door. Everyone who liked cats in the "Senior Retirement Community" asked about Apolonia.

"Very well about the ghost," replied Margie. "But she got hold of another of my prescription pills the other day. Lucky for me, she had no reaction again. I found the empty capsule the next day. I really am careful, so don't yell at me," she begged.

"I hate cats," said Frieda. "One chased my dog out into the street when I was a girl and it was hit by a car."

"Was it a big dog?" asked Annie.

"Well, yes, but it was afraid of cats, although it did maul the cat in the next apartment house."

"Were the cats friends? Sounds like a revenge killing to me," muttered Dot.

"Do any men ever sit at this table?" asked Frieda, changing the subject. "I like conversations men have. They talk about guns and high finance." She was looking at Ike's table, although she had to turn her head around to do so. Ike worked his magnetism on women without them even seeing him apparently. Frieda indicated Ike's table.

"You could ask for that table as a guest and try it out, I guess," said Carolina.

"Ike has a girlfriend," said Margie.

"Really! Did I say I was looking for a boyfriend?"

Margie, in her embarrassment, reached for her tea cup which knocked over the center vase which fell towards Frieda and sent a stream of dirty water into her lap.

"Ach!" said Rita, jumping out of her seat. "What a mess! Look at my clothes!" She looked with disgust at Margie and ignored the women who were handing her napkins. Frieda turned her back and left.

The next day, they saw Frieda seated with two men who ate at a table for four by themselves. The group saw Frieda leave the men in a huff before dessert.

"She should have asked us for advice about that table. Both of those men hate women," commented Margie.

They saw Frieda go from table to table looking for interesting men with interesting conversation for months. She never made it back to their table.

CHAPTER 5: PERFECT PAULA

Several days passed with just the five of them, or four or three, depending on visits from various friends and children, or outings. They lamely tried to bring purses and canes and eyeglasses to make the table look full again. But the day came when another woman, this one meticulously dressed in a pale silk suit, admired by Rita, came and introduced herself. "My name is Paula. Is this my seat?" She frowned a bit at not facing the dining room but then she smiled. She listened as they all introduced themselves and knew their names from then on. That achievement was Olympian in this setting.

She said, "I'm going to like it here." She ordered without fuss and thanked the server. She ate without complaint, although she was not given the right vegetable nor served water that she had requested. She rarely made conversation, but listened well and sympathetically to all complaints.

With Margie at the table, there were complaints. Something was always going wrong for Margie. The woman attracted bad luck.

But Margie had nothing on their old tablemate, Lillian, for complaining. Carolina wondered how even she could have stood Lillian who had declared (correctly) at EVERY meal, "This is NOT food!" and then went on to describe why in detail in an outraged tone. Anyway, Paula was now in Lillian's old seat. Lillian had gone on to a better place. Really, a better place—her son's home. Upon her arrival, her daughter-in-law had immediately been forced to take a course in gourmet cooking. While she was living there, Lillian had served as a good deterrent to interlopers trying to invade their table. For some reason, she and the others at the table had slowly grown fond of Lillian.

Paula shamed the table into being on their best behavior even though she never gave even a whisper of criticism. Dinner went well but seemed very long.

They said good-night with relief and left the dining room quietly.

In the elevator with Carolina, Annie said, "How do you like Miss Perfect?"

"I do," said Carolina. "What's not to like?"

"Give me the cat hater or the pincher back."

"She does make dinner long, doesn't she?"

"You're mannerly, Carolina, and a bit prissy but you don't make us feel like bad schoolgirls who should behave better. Why is that?"

"She certainly doesn't say anything critical or even imply it. But I know what you mean."

"My floor," said Annie.

"What do you mean 'I'm prissy'?" said Carolina to Annie's back as the elevator door conveniently closed.

Three seemed to be the charm for any more additions to the table. Paula stuck, to the disappointment of the other five. They all seemed to be wilting under her politeness and good grooming. Margie started to look even dowdier, her wig losing the rest of its curl; Annie's delightful joy of life was dampened; Dot wore depressing black felt hats, and Rita started buying compulsively from the internet again. Carolina found she was blaming herself for not achieving the goal every mother but hers had tried to set for their daughters in the old days—being a perfect lady in manners, voice and dress—like Paula.

Paula was out one day, having properly notified staff and dining companions. That gave the five friends a chance to talk among themselves at dinner and try to get back their old camaraderie and fun.

Margie said, "I'm ready to move. Maybe not now, because I like being with all of you. But I keep eating more to get over the frustration of not being good enough when I eat with Paula."

"Overeating is not a productive solution, and your son is not ready to spend lots of time with you, Margie. The problem is, what can we do about Paula?" said Carolina at her bossiest.

"Maybe she can find us talking about how to get rid of her. It worked before," said Dot.

"You saw how that worked. We still have Mike to deal with," said Rita.

"In the past, we've tried crowding them out, suggesting other tables they might like better, hiding out (indicating Margie) and leaving the problem for Management to solve. What else can we try?" asked Dot.

"We can move to another table, eat at the later seating, or give her the silent treatment. But that would be unkind and those strategies might backfire. The residents here might dislike us even more. It's cowardly. She's our cross to bear for some reason." This analysis came from Carolina.

"Show us your hair shirt, Carolina. We don't like to suffer, especially at our age. We want to enjoy the time we have left." Dot was really grumpy tonight.

"Paula really doesn't say anything offensive," Annie added, siding with her best friend Carolina on principle.

"Maybe we should start dropping things on her favorite clothes. It worked with Frieda. I mean, does Paula go to the dry cleaners every day?" said Rita who looked like her own expensive clothes could use a little ironing. She felt a pang of guilt towards Margie about the "dropping things" remark. "Sorry."

"Let's get her a friend," suggested Carolina. "Some people here prize clothing over everything else. Paula looks great in her clothes—probably a size 0. We can eat away from this table more often, and ask the Dining Room manager to put the few of us left on those nights, including Paula, at somebody's table we think might try to 'steal' her. And don't look for greener pastures yourselves!"

They looked around the dining room.

"There's often a place at Beverly's new table since she moved. But Beverly might be jealous because Mike sits there now. Other women are jockeying to be near Mike. Beverly has held them off until now," observed Dot.

"Let's try Joan's table. She'll talk about shopping at Lord & Taylor's, and they might be happy together. Joan babbles and Paula is quiet and polite," replied Carolina.

"You mean deadly," said Margie. "Who'll talk to the Dining Room manager to put us there when we are short at our table? We have to plan when to be out together so they will move Paula for a night. The manager likes to put residents who bring guests at this table when most of us aren't here. "

Plans unfolded. Carolina felt uncertain about the plan but they felt the need to do something. It was a relief to stop paying intense attention tonight to eating properly and to manners as they had been forced to do in recent days since having Paula with them. They watched other tables as various people went over to Mike, shaking his outstretched hand.

"Is he running for something?" asked Margie. "The resident representative position on the Courte's oversight committee is filled."

"He may be politicking to ostracize us even more and to be in a position to meet more women to manhandle," said Dot.

"Are more people avoiding all of you?" asked Carolina.

"Yes," they all agreed.

"I get sarcastic comments too," said Margie, the most vulnerable. "Frieda is the worst."

"We have to be friendlier to people now," said Carolina. "Who's going to Mike's party tomorrow?"

"I don't want to," said Margie.

"None of us do," replied Carolina.

"I want to," said Rita.

"I like those coffee and cake parties. Sometimes they have appetizers," agreed Annie. "I wonder if they'll have those little frankfurter things in pastry. Everyone likes those." She and Rita were ready to party.

"I wonder if they'll ever have a vacation theme like Bermuda or something," Rita said wistfully.

Margie looked struck, probably remembering where her ex had celebrated the date of their divorce with some woman on a cruise.

"Well, just don't get your backside too close to Mike," advised Dot, "unless you want him to cop a feel."

Carolina volunteered her sage advice again, "We all need to go and wish Mike well. I never saw anyone affect a large group of people he didn't know like Mike has."

"That's why. They don't know him," said Dot.

"His true colors will become known," said Carolina.

"Maybe more women here enjoy being felt up than I realized," said Dot, looking daggers at Annie and Rita.

"That's a funny time they have for a party," said Margie quickly—ignoring her comment, "right before a four course dinner."

"They're having wine too, to toast," said Annie. "My children had a cake for our table on my 90th birthday, remember?"

They ended dinner by agreeing to meet at quarter to three to go to Mike's party the next day and to be out somewhere for dinner on the day following that so that Paula would be forced to be seated at another table. Rita volunteered to mention to the Dining Room manager that Paula had asked to sit with Joan when their table was not going to meet for dinner.

CHAPTER 6: IT'S PARTY TIME, DAMMIT

The next day, they entered the dining room that was decorated with a flower at each place setting as a gift, and a banner overhead that proclaimed WELCOME MIKE! Carolina thought it should have had a disclaimer on it: "Paid for and Approved by Mike to Get Even with the Table in the Corner."

"Let's break up and schmooze at separate tables," whispered Rita.

Margie, out of panic, followed Carolina.

Annie, who was comfortable anywhere, with anyone, sat at a group with some of the people who went to the movies that the Courte showed at night and with a matinée at noon. She was received well.

Rita sat with Loretta, a heavy-set woman who usually bossed around whomever she could. She had a retinue as usual, drawn to her by some sort of social manipulation, but there was a space available.

Dot sat at a table with Ike and his new girlfriend, the sedate dark horse who had come from an established table and suddenly began kissing Ike in public. Nobody had noticed those vibes between them before. They said hello to Dot but were not that welcoming, being good friends of Mike.

Carolina and Margie sat at one of the front tables that had two people at it. No one said anything after Carolina said hello. However, they soon found that they were sitting in the lion's den. Mike was being introduced in front of the room by Angie, one of the workers who were assistants to Management. Mike greeted the people assembled—a full house. His new best friend, Beverly, stood beside him. He was saying, "And a fine lot of people you are too, barring some. You would make darlin' Irishmen. Drink up!" Angie made the toast while drinks were handed to Mike and Beverly. The glasses of champagne for the rest of them had been served while they were waiting. Mike and Beverly then made their way to their table—and straight for Carolina and Margie. Margie looked like she was going to bolt. Carolina put her hand on Margie's arm. "Smile," she whispered. Mike kept his genial smile and held the chair for Beverly who was seated next to Mike, who took the seat next to Carolina. Carolina looked for knives on the table but was reassured when she saw that there were only forks for the Irish Whiskey Cake and spoons for the coffee.

The welcomes started. The two friends of Mike shook his hand. Carolina said, "Yes, welcome to our community, Mike." Mike put out his hand and Carolina had to shake it. She felt a tremor of hatred from Mike's eyes that went to his hand then to hers. She'd hardly ever felt hatred like that in her life. She knew fear. This man was out for revenge. How far would he go?

Margie said, "Yes, welcome," and lifted her cup for the server to pour her coffee. Her hands were full so she escaped Carolina's ordeal.

Beverly said, "Some people have no right to be eating the cake and drinking the coffee Mike has so generously provided. They should choke on it if there was any justice."

Mike said, "Forgiveness is a virtue. Even the people on that Green Isle live in peace now."

"The cake is very good, Mike. Thank you," was all Carolina had to say.

"Yes, thank you," whispered Margie, looking down. Margie felt guilty about everything everyone ever thought she should feel guilty about.

People started coming around to wish Mike a personal welcome before they left. They looked with surprise but acceptance at Carolina and Margie. Mike stood up and politicked like an Irish mayor at an old St. Patrick's Day Parade.

People who had ostracized Carolina came over to be friends again, thinking all was forgiven by Mike. Carolina and Margie escaped into the crowd. By some instinct, Dot and Rita nodded like they were best friends with Mike as they passed his table unobserved by him, following Carolina and Margie out.

In the waiting area, everyone who left said greetings to Carolina's group. The Dining Room manager came out to break up the group to end the gridlock in the aisle around the turn to the elevator and the concierge desk.

Carolina's group walked on to the mailboxes. Margie whispered, "Did it work?"

"I think so," said Carolina. "Just act like we love everyone, as we should. But stay away from Mike, especially in dark halls when you are alone."

"Why?" said Dot. "Is he going to grab asses again?"

"Shhh! Don't ruin what we started," said Rita, shocked.

"Let's get out of here while we can!" begged Margie.

"It's almost time for dinner. We have to go in soon," said Annie who had joined them. She wandered off to the library, pausing to see if Floyd had somehow materialized from Florida in the music room, but had to settle for talking to another group. Annie could always find friends.

The rest left for a little while, then returned for dinner, which went as expected, with Paula there. Everyone was nice to them again as they came and left.

They dispersed to their rooms to plan for the next day when they would be absent from their table. Rita had had a word with the Dining Room manager about Paula's imaginary request to sit with Joan.

Margie was the only one with a bad experience, passing Frieda who said loudly to whomever was there, "Some people should not be allowed to have cats here, especially sloppy people who smell up the place."

CHAPTER 7: THE STATE OF ENNUI

The table reassembled the day after next, Paula sitting contentedly with them again. She said it had been agreeable to sit at another table for a change but she was glad to be back. The rest looked disappointed. Rita and Margie especially drooped.

Carolina philosophically thought it was nice to be liked. She replied politely and thought to herself that they should pay for the social sins they had made with Mike. Carolina was a bit holier than thou at times.

They ate in misery, except for Paula who seemed fine.

"You didn't come down for Mike's party, Paula," said Annie, who was the only one with the energy to talk to her now. Paula somehow sucked out one's energy. "The whiskey cake and champagne were good."

"I was busy. I saw the pictures of it up on the bulletin board by the mail boxes. Carolina and Margie looked very good there. Mike was holding Carolina's hand."

"Have you moved your furniture yet?"

"No, I'm keeping this furnished apartment for a while."

The others perked up, hoping there was a reason behind Paula's temporary status.

"You weren't in the flood, were you, Paula?"

"No, but I need time to reorganize my things." She ate quietly, not volunteering any more information. Maybe she had nothing to say. They felt the vibe not to ask her anything although Paula was maybe just being herself, the woman who wasn't there.

Carolina was wondering if Paula's lack of identity was because she had been squashed as a girl. Girls were squashed when she was young, although Paula was a bit younger than Carolina. At least, a ladylike blank was better than someone who hated them like Mike.

Margie recounted her story of Frieda's mean remarks to her friends and received sympathy in the form of: "It's not you, Margie. It's her." And "Your cat is very lucky to have you, Margie." And "You are spotless in your apartment." And "Ignore her."

"I'll bet you were glad to get me after Mike and Frieda," said Paula with a vacuous smile.

Various unenthusiastic responses included: "Uhm, yeah;" "Of course;" "Sure;" and "How lucky can we get?" Carolina thought the last remark went a little too far into sarcasm.

After dinner when Paula left, Carolina told the others that she thought they just had to accept Paula and hope she would leave. If any one of them could not stand it any longer, they could temporarily switch to the later seating. Margie especially looked bedraggled and pushed to her limit between dealing with Paula and Frieda.

Trying to encourage her friends, Carolina told them in a tone meant not to carry to other tables, "See that man over by the first pillar? No, don't all look at once! Well, I heard the Dining Room manager was trying to have him put here before we got Paula. He asks for the food the others don't finish on their plates and picks his teeth with a toothpick, a used dirty toothpick! He keeps talking about ways to save money too. Someone told me he's so miserly that he'd be happy if Tiny Tim died so he could finish Tim's plum pudding. You know I don't like to gossip, but I wanted you to know why I said Paula should be accepted. She seems nice, just boring."

The others looked like they were seriously considering the choice, but didn't say anything to Carolina about preferring Mr. Scrooge.

Life settled down again. The diners never got used to Paula, but listened to more of Carolina's lectures on being grateful they didn't have to sit with the likes of Rolanda or Wanda anymore as some of them had had to in the old days.

"I'm still not going to join your nunnery, Carolina," Dot had told her recently. "You suffer cheerfully if you like."

Rita started buying stuff and then discarding it in the trash room again, her meticulously pressed self of old looking wilted; Dot bought even more hats she couldn't afford; Annie lost her sparkle; and Margie looked like a wild animal ready to bolt. She couldn't sit still. Carolina did not believe in all of this online buying to solve problems, but knew she had to shut up or be called St. Carolina. As for Paula, in her designer clothes she shone as the moon at their table, but Agatha Christie had once pointed out in one of her mysteries that some preferred the sun. They all longed for any kind of eclipse.

Mike and Beverly continued to make sarcastic remarks about them, but the place settled down to tolerating both camps. Many did not understand why Mike had been so friendly to them at his party, so thought he might be flighty, and the others who knew what had happened appreciated the joke played on him. They liked Carolina and Rita and Annie a lot and had finally remembered it.

Carolina still waited for Mike to make his move, although round two had gone to the colleens.

Annie pointed out to Carolina that Mike at least had never asked her "North or South?" when she introduced herself, the way most men did.

"That's true. That's really true. I'll try to remember it when I see him in an empty corridor." (Carolina had been named for two aunts—Caroline and Ina, but not for any of the Carolinas. She was a Quaker Yankee born and bred in Pennsylvania.) She remembered the day she'd been asked to stand for the playing of "Dixie" down south and beat herself up for not asking for the "Battle Hymn of the Republic" to be played too.

Put old battles to bed, she told herself. *Enjoy the Lord's gifts you have today.*

She looked up from dinner and out the window to see the local grocery truck delivering someone's groceries. Margie, who had the twenty-five meal dinner plan used it the most. The rest had the full month's plan and shopped only for lunch foods and snacks. Dot, Rita and Carolina all used the grocery service, but not often. "I hope that's not for you, Margie."

"No. I can't be in two places at once. My delivery window is later."

"You'd be surprised how many people make that mistake and are not home when they're supposed to be. They get charged a fee," said Dot.

"I'm careful. I use the grocery delivery truck for food, mail delivery for cat supplies and direct pharmacy delivery for prescriptions and health supplies. I need them all. I will even need them if I live near my son someday since he's so busy."

"Yes, your child is younger by about 20 or 30 years than the rest of us who have children," said Annie. My children now have time to get things for me. (Neither Dot nor Carolina had married nor had children.)

"The pharmacy now requires that you sign for delivery these days. You have to sign at the desk if the pharmacy guy doesn't take it to your apartment. The concierge doesn't bring up prescriptions anymore. I wonder if there was a mix-up that made them change," said Dot.

"The Management does keep secrets sometimes," replied Paula knowingly.

"Not from some of the men. It's easy for the men to get cozy with the concierge. They sit behind the desk with him and read the paper," said Annie. "But the women here are too old for most of the concierges who are afraid we old girls are making a play for them."

"What services do you use, Paula?" asked Carolina to include her.

"Nothing yet. I do use the mail and UPS for my moving."

"I heard some people are getting tired of Mike. He's wearing out his welcome in some areas. Pinching is not always valued here," said Rita.

Annie nodded. Annie had friends who talked too.

Carolina tried to change the topic. "Are any of you doing anything new we should know about? I myself am going to work at my church's block party again." Carolina went to her church almost every Sunday where the congregation was like her family. One family from it even had her beloved pets and would have taken Carolina in, but she thought preserving her independence was best for her and for them.

"I'm writing an article for the Courte's newsletter this month," said Margie unexpectedly.

"Good," beamed Carolina. "What's it about?"

"I was asked to write about spring. I started it already. It's called: 'Enjoy Spring. How Many of Us Will Be Here for the Next One?'"

Dot laughed; Annie choked; Rita sputtered; and well-mannered Paula coughed to hide her glare.

Carolina said, "No! You can't. Write about the robins or how we all feel young in spring. I'll give you some poems to quote. We're unpopular enough."

"So are we a PR firm now?" asked Margie, with unusual rancor.

"No, but that's an unkind theme except in church, Margie, where it would be appropriate at funerals."

"You write it then," said Margie."

Everyone looked shocked.

"I'm sorry, Margie," said Carolina. She knew she'd said something wrong to upset Margie so much, or else something was wrong with Margie. Either way she should be quiet and think about things before she said them.

"I'm sorry too," said Margie. "I know you're trying to help. I just heard from my ex last night about some piece of business we still had to settle."

Margie was in a space where she was fixated on her ex-husband and the home she had lost. She had improved in the last few months but backslid from time to time, like now.

"Forget infidelity these days. Hiring a hit man to kill you AND being unfaithful is the new bad," Dot said philosophically.

They all looked at her in surprise.

"Since when are you watching true crime shows?" asked Rita.

"For a while. I guess I'm bored."

"I should have known we weren't compatible when I caught him on the Ayn Rand dating site.

He would get so mad at me for watching 'The Daily Show' and 'Colbert.'" I thought he was a registered Democrat until the last few years of our life when he loved Fox News." Margie was flashing back again. "I remember a woman saying something about how her first great love for her husband was mixed with resentment after fifty years together."

"I understand that," said Dot, who'd never married.

Rita and Annie, who both missed their beloved late husbands, didn't understand.

"I was thinking about Shakespeare's *Hamlet* when I remembered that line about the slings and arrows of outrageous fortune. That is what happened to you, Margie. Your husband was an arrow of outrageous fortune. It happens to all of us, in different forms. We expect our misfortunes to be within limits, but when they come they sometimes aren't." Carolina thought a lot about Shakespeare's lines and applied them to everyday life.

"Exactly," said Margie. "That makes it easier to understand and accept. I wanted to go to a feminist retirement home but couldn't find any. This place is just as good sometimes."

"Of course, it's as good as that mythical place you dream of." This time it was Dot who started to preach instead of Carolina. "You could make more friends, Margie, if you thought about how things look to other people. You were sitting outside reading *The Communist Manifesto* with everyone going by."

"For educational purposes! I'm studying Russian history. I had to finally buy the book. Libraries don't seem to replace stolen copies these days. You know I read historical books and watch documentaries."

"But think how it looked. Everyone avoided you, I saw them. I did too."

Annie said, "How could you, Margie? It's like reading a book by a ... a communist."

"The people here are old enough to remember the Cold War and the Russian scare with Cuba and the invasion of Poland by the Russians like it was yesterday. You should have read it in private," said Carolina, "for your own sake."

"But I can't be intellectually dishonest, can I?"

"Yes!" was heard from four other voices.

"Oh! Then should I tell people that I only read *The Communist Manifesto* for educational purposes?"

"Shhhhh!!!" The others looked at each other thinking that Margie would never learn.

"The food was healthier today," said Rita, changing the subject.

Margie wasn't finished. "My ex ate extra virgin olive oil. It was the only time in his life that he was looking for anything virgin."

The others laughed in an embarrassed way.

"I hear Floyd is coming back soon. He stayed longer to see the horses at Hialeah or wherever that racetrack is in Florida," said Annie excitedly.

"I was watching *Destination Tokyo* the other day and I thought of Floyd. The pilots in it were looking at a map of the Pacific, comparing an island surrounded by water to a man totally surrounded by women," said Margie. "You know, like Floyd."

Annie looked decidedly miffed, not liking to hear Floyd described that way.

Apparently, Floyd had reminded Margie of her ex and her divorce. "They say what doesn't kill you makes you stronger. I think that's dumb. It can make you weaker and be broken too."

"Shall we leave?" asked Annie, having heard enough from Margie in one of her overly talkative moods.

"That sounds good. I have to wait for my groceries. The concierge knows to let the driver in. And the pharmacy may send my stomach medicine over. My digestion is upset lately," said Margie, although it didn't show in what she had scarfed down for dinner.

They left, still with a mood of oppressiveness and dissatisfied gloominess upon them, getting on each other's nerves more than ever. And Paula had hardly said a word.

CHAPTER 8: ATTEMPTED FELINE MURDER

Carolina woke to the sound of her telephone. She sat up in bed and answered. It was Margie on the phone.

"Please come down, Carolina. Apolonia is unconscious."

"I'll be right down."

Carolina threw on a blouse and skirt and removed the net that preserved her perfect waves in their old fashioned hairstyle her mother also had worn. She hurried down the stairs.

She opened Margie's door which was unlocked and went to Margie's bedroom where Apie was on the bed.

Margie cried, "Help her please, Carolina."

"Call the vet. Look for a pet hospital if you don't get an answer. Call a cab. Call the concierge if you need help."

Carolina bundled Apie up in a blanket. She told Margie to put on day clothes. Margie had called a place that advertised all night emergency service. Carolina went up to get her purse with money.

They rushed downstairs and got in the cab which did not object to the cat. They got to the hospital and the cat was whisked away after it was determined that Margie didn't know what was wrong with Apie, and they had ascertained that someone would pay. The two waited for hours after they had left Carolina's credit card for the cat's treatment.

Carolina and Margie sat alone. After Margie gained some control over her crying, Carolina asked if Apie had been shocked or fallen or eaten something to injure her.

"I don't know. I fed her before I went to bed and woke in the middle of the night to find her like you saw her."

"What did you feed her?"

"That was funny. My groceries came after dinner but the canned cat food I'd ordered wasn't in the bags. I gave her part of a bag of tuna fish; you know, it comes in those pouches."

"Did it smell odd?"

"No, it smelled OK."

"Did she play with any plugs?"

"Not recently. She's improved in our new apartment. She's so beautiful, Carolina. My beautiful calico cat."

"I agree. She is beautiful. I love her green eyes and black and orange-colored fur."

"And her tail. When her tail is out straight and you can't see the rest of her body, it looks like a big sleek snake. It's twice the size of other cats' tails. She fights with it sometimes when it gets in her way. I love her so much."

"I know." Carolina missed her own cats and dog who now lived on a country estate with a family of friends who had children. She saw them as often as she could. She knew they were happy there but agonized over whether she had done the right thing. She was convinced they loved the new home but missed her. She felt they needed to be with each other though.

The doctor came out asking where the cat could have gotten the food she'd eaten. It was poison. They were sending a sample out to be analyzed.

"Did the cat go outside?"

"No, I gave her tuna fish a few hours ago."

"We think she'll be OK. Are there other animals who might eat any food there?"

"No."

"You should go home. She's asleep. Come back anytime after nine tomorrow."

After signing some more papers, they called a cab and left.

"Who would hurt Apolonia?" asked Margie.

"Get some rest, Margie. We'll talk tomorrow at eight. By the way, only eat what isn't opened and nothing in light plastic or pouches. OK?"

"OK," said Margie in alarm but ready to fall down from stress and fatigue.

"Put your chain up."

Carolina went to her apartment. She checked it for intruders, telling herself she was paranoid but forgiving herself under the circumstances, knowing more than Margie how serious the situation was. She sat down at her desk and made a list of things to do. She finally put her old fashioned flannel nightgown back on and went to bed.

Morning came early. She got ready and went to Margie's apartment. Margie was ready.

"Did you sleep at all, Margie?"

"Not really. I didn't take my pill since it was too late."

"Could Apie have gotten hold of some of your pills?"

"She eats anything, even her kitty litter sometimes when it's fresh. Since she was an abandoned kitten, the shelter kept kitty litter in the basement for treatment to keep her away from other cats. She was down there in a cage for months. I didn't find any half-eaten capsules on the floor like I do when she gets them. I'm very careful now. I open the plastic pill containers over a drawer."

They left for the animal hospital, this time being driven by the Courte's driver. Everyone was very solicitous of the pair since the concierge on duty had reported their visit to the animal hospital in the middle of the night. The local theory at the Courte was that Margie had poisonous plants that Apie got into, but that wasn't true.

They were met by the vet in the hospital and led to Apolonia who was awake but hooked up to an IV. Margie held her softly. After a while, the Doctor took them aside and said, "It was poison for sure. They are working on the type now. Do you want the police involved? How do you think she got it? Here's a number you can call if you think of anything."

Margie looked terrified. She was petrified of being accused of hurting her cat and losing her. She didn't think someone was trying to kill the magnificent little cat. Having nothing to offer the doctor, they went to sit on a bench outside of the office.

"We have to go to the police, Margie."

"No, please. I'll get my ex-husband to take her. She will be subjected to smoke and awful women and other animals that might bully her there, but she will be safer."

"Not yet, Margie. We can keep her safe. She needs you. Maybe my friends can take her with my pets on their estate for a while. But she would go outside and that may make apartment life difficult for her."

Margie bent over crying. "Why is my life so awful now? A neighbor in my old condo said I attract this misery to myself. I don't seem to be able to get any good luck, even neutral luck, except for meeting people like you and Annie."

"Buck up, Margie. You seem to be the Pauline in peril these days, but we will save you again."

Margie looked up smiling. "I will change my name to Pauline. Please, please help me, Carolina."

"You can stay in my extra room tonight. We'll talk and then decide what to do."

Carolina called Annie, Dot and Rita to her apartment when they got back. They sat with Margie and discussed the circumstances.

A call came to Margie on her cell phone. "Anti-freeze?" She hung up. "Anti-freeze and some sleep medication they think. But Apie did not eat enough to kill her."

"Do you think it would have been enough for a person if she ate it all?" asked Dot.

"I don't know," said Carolina. "It could have been meant for Margie. It could have been lethal mixed with the medications she takes. We have to go to the police."

"They'll put me away in prison again," said Margie fatally.

"For trying to poison yourself?" said Annie.

"My cat almost died, not me."

Carolina asked Margie, "How did you get the tuna?"

"I got the food delivery service from the grocery store tonight. You know, you order online and they come within some scheduled hours to deliver it. They have to come in from the side door or else come in the middle entrance and go by the concierge's desk. Sometimes the concierge calls me that a delivery is coming and sometimes the service itself calls me to let them in the locked side door. This time the concierge called me from the desk."

"The tuna was in this shipment for sure?" asked Rita.

"Yes, I unpacked it. But they didn't bring the cat food cans I'd ordered. I didn't notice until the guy had left. They bring things into your kitchen, you sign for it and they leave."

"Most of us have ordered from there sometime or other," said Dot.

"Where's your receipt?" asked Carolina.

Margie got it from her purse. Carolina checked it; the cat food was on the list to be delivered but not the tuna fish.

"I called them to say the delivery person hadn't brought the cat food cans. They credit your account but don't bring it. I was going to have to go on the pharmacy trip today to get cat food." She began to laugh but Dot stopped the hysteria by saying, "Stop it. We need your help now." Margie stopped.

"The delivery man's first name is on the receipt," said Carolina. "Did you know him?"

"No, they keep sending different people."

"We have to find out what happened to the food. Did you discard the pouch, Margie?"

"No, I'll get it."

"Later," said Carolina.

"I'm very tired, Carolina."

"Go to the guest room. I have the couch made up. We'll wake you for dinner."

"I can't go down for dinner."

"OK, why don't you lie down and sleep? We'll take care of everything," she said soothingly.

The others sat and looked at Carolina for guidance.

"We have to make a police report. I'll call them to make an appointment. I have a friend there I met when we had our other trouble. Then I'll call the grocery and try to talk to the delivery man. We have to find out if the poison was meant for Margie or for Apie. Then we'll take it from there. Someone has to stay with Margie until we understand what's going on. We have to watch what Margie eats. I'll go down to Margie's apartment and check Margie's food to see what's safe, and then we'll make an appointment with the police."

"I'll stay here today," said Annie. "My son's coming tomorrow afternoon, so I'll be busy then unless you need me."

"Thanks. Everyone stay in touch. Don't say anything to anyone about this at dinner. Lock your doors like we did before." Carolina looked especially hard at Annie who was delinquent in this area and never wanted to get up to unlock her door when someone knocked so kept her door unlocked when she knew someone was coming. Being the optimist she was, she always seemed to think she might have a visitor.

Dot and Rita left. Annie went into Carolina's bedroom to watch TV while Carolina went to her father's old desk she used in her office. She used the main living room for her office since the windows went from floor to ceiling and there was lots of light and space. There was room for the reading devices she needed and her computer.

She sat down, got on the phone and got busy. She made notes of what she'd found out from the grocery. She got the key to Margie's apartment from Margie's jacket and went down to check it out. She retrieved the tuna fish pouch wearing plastic gloves and tied up the garbage. She bagged the pouch, thinking the police would not take the case seriously enough to go through the garbage. She looked around and left.

Going back to her apartment, she called the dining room to say, "Mrs. Belbuck and I are eating in my apartment. Could you bring up dinner?" The order was placed. Carolina added, "We like the food hot. Could you bring it up right from the kitchen? Should I come down and get it?"

Margie got up when dinner came. The server assured them that the food had come hot from the kitchen. It was under those little metal covers which reassured Carolina.

They ate in silence, talking a little about Apolonia. Margie was distraught but hungry. Carolina put the dirty dishes outside the door and made more tea.

A call came in to Margie's cell phone. It was the vet saying Apolonia could come home tomorrow and to bring her carrier when they came. Carolina also got a call to her apartment. It was the concierge telling her a man was there to see her.

Three people sat around Carolina's table: A pleasant man about 50 who was intelligent enough himself to respect Carolina's mind, Margie who looked terrified of being carted away, and Carolina.

Captain Linus Dereck sat at Carolina's table drinking tea from a Spode teapot and cup. He had told her once that he had been named after the character in *Peanuts*. He said that any other name, including Charlie, would have been a better choice for him.

"Even Pigpen?" Carolina asked.

"Good point," he had answered. He was now called Captain or Cap, even by his family since he'd cringed at "Linus" all of his life. Carolina served sandwiches thinking he might be hungry when he came. It was clear he had arrived before eating his dinner. He asked Margie about the tuna fish.

"I didn't remember ordering that tuna but was glad to get it when the cat food wasn't there. The service makes mistakes in their orders and often sends samples of things as a bonus or advertisement so I didn't think twice about it."

Carolina interrupted. "The tuna was meant for Margie and whomever she might have invited over."

"You got that conclusion from the tuna not being on the receipt and the cat food Mrs. Belbuck ordered not coming? Wouldn't that mean the tuna was meant for the cat?"

"No, I called the delivery service and they did not give the tuna as a free gift and they did find a bag of cat food on the truck that was supposed to be delivered. The tuna was introduced into the grocery bag after the food left the store. The delivery man said he'd had to leave some bags on the elevator since he couldn't pick them all up at once. He hadn't used his dolly since he didn't expect to have to leave some bags on the elevator when the door closed. The elevator did go to another floor. Sometime along the way someone must have dropped the pouch in one of Margie's bags. Lots of people knew Margie was getting a delivery that night. She said so at the table and told the concierge in the lobby too. They like to know when we get deliveries or guests are coming. Margie is very conscientious about following rules."

Margie looked bewildered. She sat there in her worn polyester clothes just blinking. The detective looked at her like she might be on drugs.

"Margie is very upset about her cat. We all are. We were up all night and have not caught up on our sleep. We are picking Apolonia up tomorrow."

"You kept the cat's dish?"

"Yes. I got the pouch out of the garbage using plastic gloves. Everything is as Margie left it. I tied up the garbage since it smelled."

The Captain said, "I'll have to make a report on this. Police may be here tomorrow. Are you staying here, Mrs. Belbuck?"

"Yes, but I'm going back to my own apartment tomorrow when I get Apie. She will be more comfortable there. I can as easily be poisoned up here as in my own apartment."

Carolina refrained from telling her that there were other ways to die.

"When are you getting her?" asked the Captain.

"In the afternoon."

"Please wait until we call and let you know that we've gotten what we need from your apartment. I don't think much will need to be done. Our resources are short and we may not be able to investigate a cat who didn't even die." On that discordant note he took his leave.

The police did, in fact, come the next morning and take some evidence and ask some questions.

Carolina and Margie brought Apolonia home. Rita visited and she and Carolina checked Margie's food again, and threw out anything that could have been contaminated. Margie said she wanted to rest so the friends left with warnings. "Put your chain up! Treat everyone who comes to the door with suspicion as if they were the evil Queen in Snow White."

"But I might be hungry for an apple." Margie had the last word.

CHAPTER 9: ATTEMPTED HUMAN MURDER

Carolina got back uneventfully to her apartment. She remembered the days of the flood when she had been stalked or maybe stalked. Now she feared for Margie. Well, it looked like tonight would be OK as long as Apie continued her improvement. All was ship-shape and locked up, she told herself.

She got ready for bed. She was too tired to fix her waves. She would just wear the net on her head again. She fell asleep reading *Crime and Punishment*. She woke to a red light flashing and the sound of a truck. At least it wasn't that dratted fire alarm that shook the walls and flashed strobe lights in one's eyes. She got up to look out of her front bedroom windows that faced the front of the Courte. She saw a fire truck and an ambulance and some official cars with their lights flashing on top also. It seemed to be a big deal down there, not just some poor resident who needed help in the night. She got dressed, forgetting to take off her net and went down in the nearest elevator to the hall going to the lobby. She heard lots of people talking.

She arrived just in time to see the concierge on duty, an older man who worked at the Courte as his second job, being taken away unconscious. She saw several residents: Mike, Frieda, Paula, and Loretta. They saw Carolina. Paula came over to her.

"I saw a face by my window. It was terrible, Carolina. I called the concierge desk but got no answer. I came out to find the concierge lying on the floor. Mike had just come in from outside but wasn't walking well. I didn't know what to do. Mike said to call 911. I then called Management from a number I found behind the concierge's desk. What will we do here alone? We're all alone."

"It's OK, Paula. You're not alone now."

Mike was talking to one of the men who'd come with the ambulance. The man told everyone it was OK to go back to their rooms, that he would stay until Management sent someone to be in charge. Paula went over to him to tell him about the intruder she'd seen outside of her window. She lived on the first floor.

The man said in a loud voice, "Everyone, go back to your apartments and lock your doors and windows. I will call people who will take charge and you can contact them in the morning. If you're in immediate danger, call 911 or come to the lobby. I'll stay here until someone comes."

More people came downstairs but were sent back to their apartments.

Carolina walked Paula back to her apartment and went up to check on Margie. No sound was coming from the apartment. Margie's apartment didn't face the front of the Courte where the flashing lights were so she probably hadn't heard anything. Carolina went back to her own room.

Morning came and Carolina went down to breakfast. She usually ate in her apartment but today she wanted to hear the latest news. She went to a table with one seat left and the biggest talkers in the place.

Loretta said to Carolina, "I hear you looked fetching in your hair net, Carolina."

Carolina touched her waves self-consciously. "How is Mr. Howard?" she asked. It looked like this group knew it all.

"We don't know how the concierge is," said Hazel, who followed Loretta around like a chick after a mother hen. "We heard the police are coming to investigate some of us. It might be poison."

Carolina's mind stopped. "Why?"

Loretta interrupted her entourage of one, Hazel, frowning at her for not knowing her place and taking the spotlight. "Well, they know from talking to the other concierge who was relieved by Nello—that is Mr. Howard to you, Carolina. Nello was OK when he came arrived last night, just tired. His stomach was a little upset from what he'd just eaten at home or by the flu. He's just coming around. The police called Management today and asked them to keep the desk area as it was last night. You should have seen the concierge when you came down today, sitting outside the desk in the lobby, but getting up to answer calls to the desk. They can't ignore those, you know. The police should be here soon."

"Did Mr. Howard eat anything here?" asked Carolina.

"They don't know. He always kept his lunch under the concierge desk but all or most of it was still there."

"Anyone could get at it there if he left for even just a few minutes to set up chairs or go to the restroom," said Carolina, almost to herself.

"Well, the police are coming to question everyone," said Loretta, proud to know things others didn't and happy about trouble she could talk about.

"Paula saw a face at her window—like a witch doctor's, she said. She's on the first floor. And Frieda said she saw it too. The face was lit up in the dark when she was in bed. Frieda said it tapped on her window to wake her up and made sure she looked at it." Loretta announced this like she was announcing VE Day.

Carolina took in all of this talk and got up to go see Margie. She brought Margie breakfast, braving Management's wrath to do so, who would then send out memos to everyone reprimanding them for taking food out of the dining room. (Some residents stuffed food into their purses and walker seats for their aides who seemed to enjoy eating the smashed up food or at least pretended they did.)

Margie opened her door, leaving the chain on as she checked who was there. She was in protective mode for Apolonia's sake, for whom she imagined she was the body guard, from a world that was out to murder her cat.

Reinforcements had arrived. "Oh, Carolina, come in."

"How is she?"

"Resting. She drank water. She'll be OK soon."

"Sit down, Margie. You must have been up all night with Apie. I'll make us some tea. I ate already."

Carolina fixed tea and they sat at Margie's table in the kitchenette area. Margie's kitchen had the set-up they all had of galley kitchen area, open dining and open living room, fronted by giant windows on the living room end.

Carolina said gently, "There was excitement last night. The concierge fainted or something. He was taken to the hospital. He should be OK. The police might be back to talk to you, Margie. Maybe it was poison; there's a rumor. And with what happened to Apie..."

Margie looked beaten and terrified. Carolina wept inside for the look in Margie's eyes.

"This is a good thing if the concierge is getting well, Margie. We can get to the bottom of everything now."

"I know what the police will think. They'll think I'm a serial poisoner. They'll take Apie away from me. The police will put me in jail again."

"Don't look so doomed, Margie. Of course they won't. I'll stay with you today."

"Thank you, Carolina."

"I'll need to leave from time to time to see what's happening. I hope our detective friend comes back."

The day passed. Margie spent part of it looking up articles on the internet about how to get out of and keep out of jail. Annie, Dot and Rita came by to visit. Apie got up and came out to sit on Carolina's lap. Carolina had to pick her up but at least she was walking. The cat loved Carolina.

Margie asked if she could put the TV on, not wanting to offend her guest. Carolina, who just wanted to think her thoughts and not talk for a time, agreed. Margie started to watch one of those shopping channels that was trying to sell elaborate Southwestern jewelry in turquoise and silver.

"I hate that necklace," Margie volunteered after a while. "It's so busy and the stones don't sparkle."

"I never see you wearing that style," said Carolina. "Are you buying a gift for someone?"

"No."

"Then why are you watching it so long?"

"It passes the time. It's what we do in this place, Carolina."

Carolina realized that Margie was getting some kind of pleasure in recoiling from each sales item, more even than she would have enjoyed watching items she liked. That was something for Carolina to remember when she was analyzing the motives and behaviors here. There was a lot of free time for most of the residents to fill, and one should not always judge people's motives based on what they would have done during a time when they had done things with more purpose, choosing from lots of alternatives.

Margie got tired of TV and turned it off. She had relaxed a little as she sat with Carolina, each woman now thinking her own thoughts.

Suddenly, Margie, who thought a lot about marriage since hers was over against her wishes, asked Carolina, "Why did you never marry?"

"There was no lost wartime romance or anything like that. I don't know actually," replied Carolina. "I wanted to marry a few times but the subject never came up with the right person. I had responsibilities with my parents and my aunts who were older when I was born. I had a lot to do when I was young, studying, travelling, getting jobs. By the time I was ready, every good man was taken or set in his ways."

"There must have been a few shy Mr. Chips' out there for you," suggested Margie.

"I guess not. They were all looking for Mrs. Chips from the book or maybe for Greer Garson."

"I don't believe in marriage anymore myself," Margie volunteered. "Marriage is just a contract. The different states have different rules too, like they do for their income taxes or transporting parrots. Marriage is NOT romantic. There's nothing safe or sacred about it. People break contracts, people just leave and at the worst times. There's something to those songs like 'Lucille' or about leaving 'Just When I Needed You Most' as that song title says." I think there should be personal contracts spelling out what each party agrees to. There could be a standard contract for people who want to be careless. Wait until half of them see what they get when they divorce! And they'd better not move to a state with bad divorce laws, that make them wait for years to contest a divorce. Couples can have nice ceremonies in fancy clothes if they want to, religious or not, but the ceremonies shouldn't have any legal authority. And no benefits should come with being 'married.' It isn't fair to single people or to people who can't marry legally. Give everyone access to health care though. The rest of it should be in the contracts. Lots of states have those 'no fault' divorces too like with car accidents. I mean, you don't need a license to have a car accident. Marriage was worse than a car accident to me, at least, the divorce was. Marriage is sometimes a matter of life or death. People should be warned just as they would be if they had to make an individual contract with another person. Maybe if people want to keep marriage traditional then they should be forced to stay in it, at least if the woman wants that. There would be less work for the government too, wasting their time on recording marriages and divorces when they don't mean anything—at least the marriages don't."

"But more work for lawyers," said Carolina, understanding how Margie had come to feel as she did, however scrambled her arguments. She'd been too old and too sick to handle her divorce, after all those years. A decent man wouldn't have put her through it, thought Carolina.

"Lucille shouldn't have left, especially with all of those hungry kids," lamented Margie.

Just then, Annie came back with the news that the police thought the concierge had been poisoned or at least they were acting like it. They had found out from the concierge that he had not eaten his lunch. He'd only taken some stomach medication for an upset stomach. He was afraid the stomach flu was going around.

Annie was sitting on the couch beside Margie and Carolina was sitting on the recliner across from them with Apie.

Margie looked funny, her face looked all distorted or something odd.

Carolina asked her what was wrong. Apie jumped down and ran to hide in the back bedroom, sensing another storm was coming.

"I ordered stomach medicine and eye drops to be delivered from the pharmacy yesterday, since the delivery person comes with prescriptions almost every day," said Margie. "You know we all have accounts set up. They bring over-the-counter medications too. I didn't get my order yesterday. I just realized. I forgot to tell the police. The concierge didn't call for me to come down to get them at the desk yesterday, and the delivery man didn't come to my door."

Now Carolina looked like the doom had come upon her too. "I have an account too. Tell me about your order."

Margie said, "I told you all I know."

Rita arrived at that moment to relieve Carolina. Carolina went to her apartment. She called her detective friend. She was surprised to actually get him so quickly on the phone. She had given the first person who answered her name.

"Captain, there's a problem here. Our concierge fell ill last night. We heard it might be poison. Can you tell me?" There was a pause. "So, it's not your case. Well, you see Margie ordered stomach medicine and eye drops from the pharmacy. They're usually delivered to the desk, but Margie just realized that she didn't get them yesterday. We heard that the concierge who fell ill said he'd taken only stomach medicine and hadn't eaten. I don't think he'd take a resident's item though, do you? I just thought you should know and might want to come over to talk to us. OK. The detectives will be here today. May I stay with Margie when she's being questioned? She's distraught. I hope the same detectives don't come as the last time when they took her to jail. Please. She might jump from her window. No, I didn't mean that. She won't. I'll be in her apartment when they come. Maybe I should call her lawyer."

Carolina went down to the concierge desk to talk to the one on duty before she went back to Margie's.

"I can't talk about it," said Arvid, who was young—most of them were young. "They did search the concierge area; that's all I can say."

Carolina went up to Margie's apartment, thinking she might have to take her to a hospital or do something medical. How much more could the poor woman take? She went in the unlocked apartment to find Margie on the bed with Apie.

"You left the door opened," said Carolina gently. "I'm sure I left it locked and Rita would have too."

"I didn't want to get up to answer it over and over so I unlocked it. I never want to get up again. They'll take Apie away and put me in jail like the last time if we aren't killed first. What's the use?"

Carolina got a chair and sat next to Margie. Margie's phone rang. Carolina answered it.

"OK. I'll tell her. I'll be down for it later."

"You have a package, Margie."

"Oh, more teapots or socks or poison. You can order anything on the internet."

"Shhhh! Don't talk like that. You'll get in trouble. You didn't do anything wrong. Act naturally or innocently at least. You need to stay here with us and Apolonia. Do you want me to call your doctor?"

"No, no. I'll be good."

A knock came on the door. Carolina opened it to find the current concierge with a package. Carolina thanked him. He looked in curiously before the door closed.

Carolina did not know what to do with the box. What if it was something dangerous? She set it in a closet and hoped for the best.

"Just a box, Margie. Try to get some rest. Do you want the radio or TV on?"

"No, I just want to lie here."

The phone rang. It was Annie asking if she could help.

"I'll call you if I need you. No, it's not good. Margie is falling apart. The police might come and talk to her."

A knock came on the door a few hours later. Carolina answered.

Two police walked in, a man and a woman, but not the same ones who'd arrested Margie before. They introduced themselves and showed I.D.

"Are you Mrs. Marjorie Belbuck?" they asked Carolina.

"No, I'm a friend. Mrs. Belbuck is lying down. She isn't feeling well."

"We'd like to talk to her."

"I'll go see how she is." After a while, Margie came out, staggering and looking like a phantom from a cemetery. Even the police seemed alarmed.

Carolina led her to a chair and they all sat down.

"We understand your cat was poisoned, Mrs. Belbuck. We're reanalyzing the items we got from your apartment."

"Yes, my cat is home now. I don't want her upset. She still has to eat or go back to the hospital if she doesn't. She almost died."

"Did you get a package from the pharmacy recently?"

"No, I ordered over-the-counter eye drops and liquid stomach antacid that includes stuff for nausea. I don't know. The pharmacist picked them out for me. They bring that kind of thing if you have an account."

"Did you ever get them?"

"No, I didn't. They are usually very efficient."

"Did you call about them?"

"No, I was too preoccupied."

"Did you find them?" asked Carolina. "The rumor must be true about the concierge then."

"We can't say," replied one of the police.

"Did the concierge wake up and tell you everything he'd eaten?"

"We can't discuss that now. We have other people to interrogate."

Margie froze at that last word.

Carolina said quickly, "A box was delivered to this apartment a little while ago. It's probably something Mrs. Belbuck ordered. She orders a lot online. Even so, I'm worried about it. I put it in the closet."

"Are you in danger, Mrs. Belbuck? Have you gotten any threats?"

"No, no. Open it if you want."

They conferred to see what they should do. They took a chance.

"Show it to us."

Carolina took them to the closet and pointed. The box had stickers on it and an address in another state as the seller. They told Margie what it said.

"That may be my socks. I use socks with my Birkenstocks."

"Birkenstocks?"

"You know, those earth shoes," she said, raising one foot to show them. "I wear them for my arches."

She got up and went to her closet. She picked up the box and tore off the tape. She opened it to show a wig.

"Oh, it's my new wig. I hope it's not too blond or red. The computer monitor doesn't always show it right. The first girlfriend my husband had was a redhead." She brought it out and put it on the table. She opened the box further and shook it upside down. "See, it's OK."

They all looked relieved.

The police left, saying they'd be back soon, if not that day. Carolina made sure the door was locked behind them.

"See, Margie, they're just asking everyone questions. You need to take care of Apolonia. I'll call down for dinner again tonight."

Margie headed for her bedroom in a state of collapse. "I can't do or think anything. My dizziness is bad today. I have to lie down."

Carolina went into another room where Margie couldn't hear and called her detective friend. He seemed wary and said he couldn't interfere. It was not his case. He sounded like he'd been warned off. Carolina wondered if she'd made any enemies in the last case.

"I can't tell you much," he said. "Yes, they did find a bag with your friend's name and pharmacy account number in it. The concierge had taken the stomach medicine. He'd been working extra hours and saw it under the desk at night, too late to call Mrs. Belbuck, he thought."

"I'm shocked. They usually don't tamper with things like that, I mean residents' orders."

"The concierge said he had to or he could not have made it through the night working. He intended to stop at an all-night pharmacy and replace the medication before Mrs. Belbuck asked for it the next day. The eye drops were on the receipt too. The bag was found in the garbage in the hall on the way to the elevator. It seems everything had been wiped for fingerprints. Be careful what you eat there, especially in Mrs. Belbuck's apartment."

"I'll look out for her too," Carolina replied, implying Margie was not the poisoner. "How is Mr. Howard, the concierge?"

"He's recovering. The eye drops had been put into the stomach medicine. Those over-the-counter things can be poisonous when ingested. Keep that in confidence. It's for your ears only."

"Of course. I won't repeat it unless I hear it from another source."

"Fair enough."

"Thank you."

"Stay safe. I know I can trust you."

Carolina hung up the phone, her mind in turmoil. What should she tell Margie? Carolina knew she would keep the Captain's confidence but knew the news would come out soon. She'd have to prepare Margie somehow. People would say that only Margie knew of the eye drops and stomach medicine behind the concierge desk. She wished she'd knocked on Margie's door last night so she could swear Margie had been in bed. Now she would have to convince the police that Margie was the target and was not some crazed lady serial poisoner putting poison in people's food. Better yet, she'd have to find the real killer—so far, the attempted killer.

Margie slept for a few hours, the most she'd ever slept at a time. She awoke groggy, with Apie beside her. She went toward the kitchen to find Carolina in her recliner on the way. She sat across from her on the couch.

"Would you like tea, Margie?"

"Yes."

"I'll make it. I'll make some toast for us too."

"Thanks."

They sat comfortably at the dinette.

"There may be some things, Margie, that might disturb you."

"Like what?"

"Your pharmacy order was delivered, but was disbursed to others. Don't be upset when you hear it."

"Who took it?"

"I can't talk much about it. I think you can figure that out. Who got sick? We'll hear all of the details soon. Mr. Howard is going to be fine though."

Margie was very smart. "It was meant for me. I know it. It's my fate."

"Don't, Margie, that's not so. We have to find out who is behind this. The danger seems to be confined to poison. You have to be super careful about what you eat. Dinner from the kitchen is pretty safe when we see it come from there. I don't think the person will poison everyone eating there by putting toxic substances in something served to all."

"Should I move?"

"That's up to you. It will make it harder to discover who's behind this. I can find some place for you to go if you need to leave immediately."

"No. I'll only give Apie canned food I just opened," said Margie thinking about her cat first.

"You're very brave, Margie."

"They may be after you too, Carolina, if you get too close."

"True. I have thought of that."

Suddenly, they saw a black and orange little head emerge from the bedroom. Apie walked to her food bowls and drank water. Margie jumped up and opened a fresh can of cat food—not tuna fish—putting it in Apie's bowl. The beautiful cat smelled it and tasted it while the women held their breaths. She ate a few mouthfuls and turned to go back to the bedroom. They heard her stop in the bathroom and scratch in her kitty litter.

"Can you believe listening to a cat pee can sound like celestial music?"

"No," answered Carolina, with tears in her eyes. "She will just keep getting better and better now. She's very brave too."

"She is."

CHAPTER 10: CAROLINA WEAVES A WEB

Apie did continue to improve very quickly after that.

The concierge got well and came back to the Courte on probation after writing a letter of apology to Mrs. Belbuck for stealing her medication (and thus saving her life). It turned out they had a hard time hiring anyone who would work his hours and take extra shifts on weekends too. And they were afraid he would somehow sue them for enticing him to take poisonous substances, and believed he could open a can of worms the press might exploit. A guilty and grateful worker who is magnanimously forgiven might make a better employee than one who is chastised.

It turned out the employee in question had seen the bag of Margie's medication and knew he wouldn't be able to stay until the end of his shift without the stomach medicine. He had informed the police that the medication was on an open shelf under the desk and seemed like it was packaged from the manufacturer with a round sticker on top that he had had to peel off. The receipt was stapled to the side of the pharmacy bag. He could see it was stomach medicine in the bag since the bag did not quite close on top. He had had to spend a lot of time in the bathroom around the corner from the concierge desk that night. He came back from one of his trips, took the medicine in desperation, and fell over. He didn't know anything about poison.

Mike had started to be friends with the concierges, getting his paper and reading it next to the concierge on the extra chair they had behind the desk for other workers who sometimes came in when needed. The side door of the office that led to the desk was unlocked for staff to come in and out that way during the day. Anyone could get into the offices and then come around to the very long counter/desk or they could come through the front door to the desk which was always unlocked. Not to mention that a very spry person could jump over the desk, but there was a chance that behavior would be seen by anyone coming in from the three hallways and double entrance doors. All corridors led to the concierge desk and there were at least four ways in.

Carolina decided she would sit in the library facing the concierge desk and see what activity would make tampering with a package possible. She decided to call up one or two of her friends at a time and begin using the room as an old fashioned parlor.

On her way down in the elevator, she was met by a small boy who was waiting in front of the elevator door on the first floor to see who was getting off.

He came up to her with a very serious face and asked, "Are you Mother Goose?"

Carolina was startled but did her best not to show it, while wondering how she looked to other people.

"Well, no, dear, but I know her work. She's an admirable woman." Carolina wondered if she should analyze the literary history of the Mother Goose rhymes for him, explaining to him that what American children call "Ring Around the Rosy" was actually about the black death in Europe.

Instead, she smiled and left the boy looking at the elevator for more candidates.

Carolina had forgotten that this was their first "reading da" with children in a program that travelled around visiting senior communities. She had meant to sign up for it, but had gotten sidetracked with the situation with the poison.

She had other work to do today. This was the first day she sat with the fine ladies in the crochet/sewing circle who were performing feats of complicated stitching. Carolina had only minor sewing skills. Most women of her age had learned needlework at home; she, blessedly, had had to spend little time at it, her family having a nice library and giving books as birthday and Christmas presents. But one of her aunts—Ida—had given her rudimentary lessons in stitchery. Carolina had voluntarily learned how to mend stockings and sew on buttons, but had balked after a few lessons in embroidery and crochet. She had no objection to other people learning such skills if they liked, but she had not taken to it.

Now she found herself sitting with Gretchen who had organized the sewing circle. Gretchen showed her own work to Carolina, and four other "ladies" showed theirs too.

"Tatting," said Gretchen. "Carla is doing tatting. Do you tat, Carolina?"

"No, I do some embroidery and quilting. I was hoping we might make a quilt for the poor or soldiers overseas or make baby hats for missionaries."

The others looked bewildered.

"We never thought of that," replied Gretchen. "We're doing patterns and stitches to make things to give our relations as gifts. Enid makes her own patterns. Did you bring something to work on, Carolina?" They took their work seriously. Carolina realized that sewing had gotten them through their lives as something to concentrate on as a matter of pride and as a constant activity to do in good times and bad. She wondered how many of them had done such handiwork as they sat in a sick room waiting. She felt a new respect for it and for them.

"I thought you preferred to read, Carolina," said Florence, one of the oldest residents who still looked disapprovingly on girls getting educated.

"One likes a change," said Carolina. "It's pleasant here by the fire." She looked at the fake fireplace.

"We liked to cook pheasants over the kitchen fire too," answered Florence, who was a bit deaf.

"Did you do samplers when you were young?" asked Gretchen quickly to cover the gaffe.

"No, but my Aunt Ida did. I have one of hers I'd like to show you. She did them for births and deaths, the pictures she embroidered were quite complicated. Her lettering is especially fine."

"We'd love to see them, Carolina," said Judy, a beautiful woman with white hair who looked like she'd walked out of an ad for the perfect hairstyle, but claimed to the disbelief of others that she merely washed and combed her hair. Her embroidery was exquisite as were her movements.

However, it seemed that on closer inspection, Judy seemed to be working on clothing, Carolina noticed. "I sew and mend all of my clothe," Judy said. She lifted her work which seemed to be a bra. "I sew little flowers on my underwear too when I mend anything," she added, lifting out a pair of socks and underpants from her basket. "It makes the older things seem as nice as the new things." No one seemed phased by this. Carolina nodded, thinking it was good that everyone took a practical view Judy's work.

Carolina knew Judy for her reputation for caring about others. She was just a beautiful person inside and out. Carolina, who was not much of a manipulator on the whole, wondered how they could recruit Judy for the sixth place at their table when it was available again. She would reread Machiavelli if she had to in order to plan a strategy. Judy was a treasure. But Judy was too loyal to her friends and never made an enemy and was not subject to flattery, so it was unlikely she could never be recruited or bribed. Maybe begging would help. Carolina, the dignified, was willing to stoop to begging if they could get Judy. One could only pray for a miracle.

Carolina felt like she was in a book by Jane Austen in the late 1800's where there was always a basket of needlework that had to be done, set out for ladies who needed to pass the time. She felt they should all be wearing lace caps and waiting for horses to pull up with a carriage filled with women who left fancy calling cards that required a return visit. The women doing fancy old stitching did not seem like the usual women here who'd been affected by the twentieth century, or maybe this was just their playtime. This is how they had fun. Some of them seemed to morph into women of two hundred years later in other parts of the day.

Carolina sat looking at the concierge desk. The concierge on duty was busy with people getting the Courte's memos, their newspapers and picking up packages. The concierge was not watching who was going past. He answered the phone a lot. He read between helping people, except during busy times when apparently there was no time for reading. Other staff went to their desks in the back rooms which one couldn't see from the front desk. The concierge's job was not easy, Carolina realized.

A new resident showed up saying he'd been notified that his boxes of dog food had come in. The concierge pointed behind him. The concierge watched as the resident walked through the door beside the desk and back toward the closet where shopping carts were available for those needing them to carry things to their rooms and even a dolly like porters used. The concierge helped lift the boxes if required. Another resident came by asking for her duplicate apartment key hanging on the wall near the closet in the back.

Custodians came by and sat with the concierge behind the desk on their breaks, or sat waiting to meet up with other custodians. Freddie, their boss, came by a lot. He seemed to think insulting the abilities of the residents and blaming them for every broken thing that needed repair was part of his job. His two assistants did the real work. Some residents went into the back offices to talk to Management. They had lots of time in their lives to make complaints, especially about Freddie and his procrastination, and about the quality of the food served.

Carolina worked with her sewing for a while, the close work making it especially difficult because of her poor eyesight. She knew she couldn't use this ruse for long. The sewing group met once a week and would be suspicious if she didn't show some results. The ladies' work was beautiful, although Carolina did not think the intended victim, uh, recipient, of the orange sweater done in bubble stitch would appreciate looking like an enormous pumpkin.

"I'm going to give it a green collar like leaves and have a large brown stem one can turn down

the front. Do you like this sweater, Carolina?"
Gretchen asked.

"It looks very warm and colorful." Secretly,
Carolina wondered if Gretchen was playing some
kind of elaborate joke on everyone.

"I ask my relatives to wear the gifts I make the
whole time I visit, especially during the holidays.
It makes all of this work worth it to me to see
them wearing my socks and booties and sweaters
and belts and hats. I knit or crochet all of their
clothes. I have themes sometimes. This time, I
made all kinds of fruit. Last year, I had jungle
animals as my theme. They'll look so nice in
church, and the kids can wear them to Sunday
school. Their friends are jealous, their parents say.
I'm so proud to do something for them that
impresses their friends. Children need help like
that. You know, what they call self-esteem or
something these days." She looked so contented.
Gretchen had lots of money to leave, much to the
pain of her grandchildren and great-grandchildren,
who had to do a lot to please Great Grandma
Gretchen.

The group broke up, Carolina begging off the
next week except to show her Aunt Ida's sampler
someday. They left carrying their work. Carolina
passed the concierge desk to see Mike sitting
behind it, reading a paper and greeting every
person who stopped at the desk or greeted him.

"Hiya, Mike," someone going by said.

"Top o' the mornin' to you. How's your lovely
wife?" answered Mike.

"Still half-Irish," the husband said to Mike.

Carolina went by, going to the elevator.

"Now there's a face that one never saw on the Blessed Isle," Mike said, indicating Carolina. "We there are a land of friendship and a wee drink and a bit of tickle now and then."

Carolina stopped. Was this the attack she was expecting?

But no, Mike had backed off. "But lovely she can be, Irish or not. I meant she is a strict school teacher. I tip my hat to her." He got up and pretended to tip a hat.

Carolina stood her ground, looked him in the eyes and said, "How do you know what country my family is from or if my bathtub isn't full of whiskey I make myself? Maybe I can make a still blindfolded."

Everyone around looked shocked.

Carolina smiled and walked on, going to her apartment. But she knew retribution was at hand.

CHAPTER 11: A FACE IN THE COURTE

Days followed, and sometimes one, sometimes more of the dining companions, sat with Carolina in the library, but without sewing. Annie was especially happy for their new social whirl. People sat happily with them, Carolina eliciting memories of the day the concierge left them alone in the night. Actually, that night was a pleasurable episode for most people since it had been exciting. The real fear for most of them were the faces peering in the windows.

One day, one of the eternally recurrent little "parties" at Buckingham Courte occurred. There would be drinks (one per person, hopefully, Management wished, or why else would the server be so scattered and wander away a lot from the portable bar?) and appetizers, usually little frozen store-bought pastries that had been reheated. Then an exact hour of "professional" entertainment followed, today a singer of songs from the great cultural capital of the world, Las Vegas. (The songs, not the singer, being from Las Vegas.) The library and lounge area filled up as chairs in the entertainment room were being set up by the concierge while the entertainer tested the sound system. The room was only about three times the size of a medium living room so the singers would be bombarded with shouts of "turn it down" as they sang, but still the singers set the amplifier system on loud.

Carolina came down to see Annie and Margie sitting in the library's coveted soft chairs and managed to get a seat near them. Most of the people were waiting for the doors to open to make a mad dash for the best seats in the entertainment room—a mad dash being what it is in a population of 80 to 90-year-olds with walkers.

Someone said, "It's Henry again. He sings Sinatra songs. We love Frank."

Carolina sat in a chair where she faced the concierge desk. More people came in—Dot, Rita, Frieda, Shirley, Loretta, Paula and others. Folding chairs were brought in. The line was long for wine.

Paula was saying, "I was so scared. The face came to the bottom of the windows while I was in bed. I hadn't closed my blinds all of the way so I could see a sort of devil's face through the part I could see through. I heard a throaty voice and a sound like an animal being killed in the woods, like the high-pitched sound of death. Then it was gone."

"Me too," said Frieda, whose apartment was on the first floor also. I was asleep and had gotten up to look outside for some reason, maybe a noise. I saw a glowing evil face right in front of me. It wasn't a person. I swear it."

The others shivered.

"You were all so happy to have chosen an apartment on the first floor so you could get to the dining room quicker and bragged about being able to get out of the building when the elevators were out during the flood. Most of us can get around fine now when the elevators work. Who has the last laugh now?" Mrs. Mealey, who said this, was usually sour and was avoided whenever possible. No one knew how she'd gotten such a wonderful husband. "Now you have to be afraid of being hacked to death or something worse in the middle of the night."

Annie answered, "If the spirit out there is supernatural, it can get to your room too, Mrs. Mealey, and it won't have to use the elevator."

"Yours too, Annie. You aren't on the first floor either."

"What did the face look like?" asked Carolina quickly to break up a childish fight.

"Black with red eyes and evil. It glowed like it came from hell," said Frieda.

"You only saw the face?" Carolina continued her interrogation of Frieda.

"Yes."

"Do you have bushes outside your windows?"

"Yes, they're very generous with their landscaping here."

"Was your TV or the heat on or something that makes sounds?"

"No and it wasn't that kind of sound," interrupted Paula with a shudder. "I didn't sign up for and pay so much money to live with a ghost or a demon."

"I'm not afraid of the boogeyman," said Mrs. Mealey's husband gruffly. "Silly women. You probably saw the moon between the trees, just some optical illusion." He was afraid his wife would make him move again so he was uncharacteristically out of sorts.

"Harrumph!" said his wife, "Silly old man, more likely."

"It was real," swore Frieda.

"Let's go in or we won't get a good seat," said Carolina. "I wonder why it's so busy today. Henry comes every few months to sing so it's not like he's something new."

"Maybe the residents are afraid to stay in their rooms," mumbled Dot.

"It's still odd that those faces appeared the night the concierge got poisoned," added Margie, but only Carolina seemed to be paying attention to her.

CHAPTER 12: CAROLINA THINKS

Life seemed to return to normal after a few days. People thought everything regarding the poisoning of the concierge was just an accident, as Management PR suggested, but never said. ("Don't upset the old people," was their motto.) Nobody moved out. Apie flourished.

More important, people seemed benign again after everyone had seemed sinister for a while. Now the polite were polite; the grumpy, just grumpy.

The season got warmer. Residents started to sit on the outdoor benches and a few had little parties in their apartments. They talked about the cards they'd all received in their mailboxes, saying "Save the Date" for a spectacular party called "Celebration Day at the Courte." They waited in suspense for information on it to follow. Then they forgot about it.

At dinner one day, Annie told the table that her favorite movie in the world was coming soon— Greta Garbo in *Camille*. She didn't know that Carolina, remembering this, had recently put a suggestion that management show the film in the request box.

"Let's all try to come if we can," said Carolina to everyone. "We can make it a party." She looked at Paula when she said it, trying to make her feel included.

Paula had become part of the furniture, although she didn't say much more than she had before. Her clothing still looked fresh, as if she were some sort of personality on local TV. Rita started to look well turned out again too. The others' problems lessened. The diners talked around Paula, since she didn't say much, but was politeness itself. She was very helpful at the table, offering condiments or an extra spoon if someone needed one. She explained how the menu worked if a new resident sat at their table when one of the regulars was gone. She was good for the table in other ways. None of the workers would ever think of disturbing a person who looked like she could be at an afternoon party with the old queen by taking her table cloth away. And Paula helped the workers by keeping track of the time, and reminding other diners ever so carefully when it was time to let the next seating inside. One night, when Paula wasn't there, Annie said, "So Paula seems to be kind and doesn't say much. She helped me read a letter with bad handwriting I'd just received when I was in the library the other day."

"She's still boring," said Dot.

"Maybe it that we just didn't know her well that made her seem so plastic," said Carolina.

"I wouldn't go that far," said Dot.

Carolina added, "She was a pall at first. She seems to like us now and gives the impression that she's happiest when she's with us."

"I still wish we had Lillian, even with her 'This is NOT food!' comment every day. I miss her more every day," said Annie.

"I don't know. I guess we could do worse than Paula," admitted Margie.

"You say that like she was a husband," grumbled Dot. "I still wish she'd go away."

"Most of us had a rough time at first until we fit in somehow. We should give her a chance. It is nice to have her away for a day though," sighed Carolina.

"You could say that about all of us," laughed Annie.

Carolina seemed thoughtful about Paula being accepted as one of them, or nearly so. She thought about asking all of her table mates over to her apartment for tea, to seal the deal.

"Did you notice that Mike was not the life of the party at the last entertainment? The women especially avoided him. It was like oil and water. They separated when they walked around him," Margie commented.

"Maybe he's up to his pinching tricks," said Dot, with satisfaction.

"There have been rumors," said Rita mysteriously. "The men still like him though. He's a good poker player."

"Beverly seems to stay away from him now. I wonder if he was playing touchy-feely too much or too little for her." asked Carolina.

"Carolina! Really!" Annie loved it when her friend reverted to her amusing, but old-fashioned brand of racy talk.

"Has Mike forgiven us, do you think?" asked Margie.

"I'm sure," replied Annie, naturally used to everyone liking her.

"Don't be so sure," warned Carolina. "Remember what I said about meeting him alone in a dark hall."

"Be afraid, be very, very afraid," laughed Margie.

Carolina was glad to hear Margie laughing even about such a violent topic and was glad to see that her deathly dark mood had changed. *Too much of a change though*, Carolina thought, *Margie needed to be careful.*

Unfortunately, Carolina was proved right. The next day, the police came knocking on Margie's door.

"Mrs. Belbuck, we're here to ask you some questions. May we come in?"

"Do I need a lawyer? Let me call my friend, Carolina."

"Is she a lawyer?"

"Well, no," said Margie, wondering what was confusing the police.

"You're not being put under arrest at this time. We want to ask you where you were at the time your groceries were delivered and how you ordered them."

"I don't remember. My cat was sick. I was thinking of her. It was awful."

"May we sit down?"

They all sat down and Margie was asked where she'd been at critical times, and why she might poison the concierge.

Margie looked shocked at the last question. "I don't know. Why would I? Why don't you find out who poisoned my cat?"

"What about you, Mrs. Belbuck? Do you know who would want to poison you, if anyone?" The policeman said this with skepticism, making it clear he thought she was the perpetrator.

"Me? I'm not someone a person anyone would want to poison. Well, maybe my ex would, but he's in another state and has forgotten I'm even alive. I have some friends at the Courte, but lots of people here don't like me. I'm not the popular type, but no one would care enough to hurt me."

"Who doesn't like you, Mrs. Belbuck?"

"I'm not sure. One lady got rid of me at her table in the dining room, but then she got killed herself. There's a woman who wears high heels who doesn't like my shoes, and an Irishman who doesn't like any of the people at our table except for the new one, Paula, and there's a woman who used to eat with us who doesn't like cats and I have a cat—and she thinks I'm sloppy too."

"Give us the names, please," was all they could think of to ask Margie after that response. They were getting as confused as she sounded, although she was not really confused in her own mind. They took down some names, but one could tell that they thought Mrs. Belbuck wasn't worth bothering about enough to poison and it was more likely that she was the poisoner.

They left with a great deal of relief, stopping to track down the movement of groceries from what the driver had said, but the whole situation was too open to track any person down unless there was some reason to investigate someone in particular. They checked out the route the medication had taken, but left still under Margie's confusing spell. They ran the names they'd gathered from her and from the staff through their database but found no arrests or warrants outstanding, at least under those names. Only one person on the list had been in trouble before for drunken and lewd behavior but nothing violent. They all seemed to be harmless old people.

Margie called Carolina who tried to calm her down. "They'll come and take me away again," she said fatefully. "I'll end my days in prison."

Carolina got off the phone, knowing she'd have to solve this mystery to save her friend again, perhaps to save more people. There was a dangerous person here at the Courte.

She sat at her desk, making her own list.

Why would Margie be targeted for murder? She obviously was the target in Carolina's mind, but other people could have been hurt with the poisoned food too. Margie could have unknowingly served the food to visitors.

But was murder intended? With the drugs most of them took, there was probably enough poison in ingredients to kill most of them, including Margie, if the drugs were mixed together.

Why was the cat food not delivered from the truck? she thought. That could have been a co-incidence. It was not uncommon for orders to get mixed up, with all of the groceries needing to be delivered in a designated time period.

What was the meaning of those faces at the windows?

Was hurting Margie a smokescreen for something? But, if so, why call attention to the place by drawing the police into it? Nobody that Carolina knew had any suspicions that the Courte was being used for illegal activities. Well, since the last time.

It made most sense that the situation involved a personal vendetta against Margie and maybe her friends, thought Carolina.

Of course, it was possible that someone did want to discredit the Courte. She'd heard that a place in a nearby town was losing residents to the Courte.

Carolina cautioned herself again that the most likely reason was usually right. The answer could be some convoluted conspiracy, but then it was something no one could probably figure out, especially if the malefactor had a deranged mind. But she had to keep trying.

Who had it in for Margie and her table friends? Just about all of Margie's friends ate at their table.

The Dining Room manager, whoever it might be at the time, didn't like their table. The current manager really liked rich men for some reason.

Did they tip extra? Maybe they didn't complain about the food and service as much as some of the ladies.

Could the staff have a mini-version of Renaissance intrigues, with descendants of the Borgias, running amok? She was getting silly now. But it would have been easy for a staff member to move the drugs around. She thought again that maybe someone did want to discredit the Courte. This possibility reminded Carolina how their dining room group had saved the Courte from a mass emigration when someone was murdered before.

OK. Go back to what was likeliest. Margie was the target for the time being. The person/persons doing this did not care if they caused the death of one or more people—maybe death was their aim——although they were rather inept.

So, who hated Margie and was inept? Maybe a new person? Or not. One didn't notice people changing here sometimes, since they were all getting a little the worse for wear—a lot worse if one were to be honest.

Carolina thought, *I must look for incipient insanity—not in her friends though. Her friends are as true and solid as ever.* Carolina knew she'd have noticed as drastic a change as that in Margie's friends.

Paula seemed to be fitting in well and seemed to like them. Mike was something else. Mike needed to be watched. He was getting cozy with the staff behind the concierge desk. Frieda seemed to be gone from their lives, except for harassing Margie. Carolina wondered why. Margie hadn't done much to her. What was a little water on one's clothes?

There were a lot of people here, including some new ones, although neither Margie nor the group of five friends seemed to know any of the new ones. At least they hadn't mentioned them and they tended to talk about daily happenings at the table. A lot of the new people were couples from the flood who intended to move out when their homes were refurbished.

Carolina suddenly had an image of Iago. She felt there was some deep hatred behind this vendetta against Margie, not a mercenary motive. She shivered. She got up and went to her coat closet and pulled out her heavy walking cane. She moved it back and forth through the air. It gave her courage. She stood even taller, although she might have to feign a slight limp if necessary when she carried it. Their foe might be very devious and brilliant—or the opposite. Use of violence often meant a weak and diseased opponent, but not always.

Maybe they should all take a house at the beach. Rental houses were cheap at this time of year. Could Dot afford to go? Carolina thought not, and they couldn't offend her by offering to pay for her. But would they want to run away anyway? The threat might be as strong when they got back or it might even follow them. The evil Queen had followed Snow White into the woods.

Each had a right to decide for herself. The group would have to talk it out.

Carolina got her phone and called her four friends, making sure no one could hear them talk on their end. She would have a secret tea party and start building a special team if they agreed.

CHAPTER 13: TEA AND SYMPATHY

A group of five gathered in Carolina's apartment. Rita came by the far staircase and Margie from the main elevator but from the first floor, stopping at her floor but not getting out, to make it look like she was going to her apartment from the elevator indicators, then going up to the top floor. The last two, who used walkers, came by the farthest elevator after taking a walk outside. They entered Carolina's apartment separately as though they were entering a hideout. They all hoped no one knew they were meeting together.

Margie had entered last, saying, "I thought I was supposed to have tried to murder somebody, not join a secret society for committing robberies or "heists" as they call them in the movies."

"We thought you were the murderer too," said Annie laughing.

"No, no," said Rita. "She was the intended corpse."

With those words, all smiles stopped.

Margie took the last seat at the table.

"I'm glad you see the seriousness of what has happened or is happening," Carolina scolded.

Margie's face looked like Bonnie surrounded by cops while she sat in a tin can of a car, or like one of Jack the Ripper's victims, hearing his steps behind her.

"Have some tea, Margie," said Carolina, this time speaking soothingly. "I made scones with clotted cream and marmalade and toast. We can pretend we're in an English tearoom, plotting our next mystery book."

Margie loved food and her body showed it.

They handled their plates and tea cups for a while. Then they looked at Carolina.

"First, I want to say that any one of us has a right to leave this dangerous place," said Carolina. "So far, only Margie has been targeted. I myself am staying to see it though. We could all rent a place on the beach for a while and come back when it's over. But, if we do that, the person could follow us or wait until we get back. We could all scatter to the winds and probably be safe, but this is our home, at least I feel that way."

"Margie," Carolina continued, "I could ask my friends to let you live for a time at their country home. We could keep it a secret and say you had gone to visit your son. I will insist you go someplace if the malefactor becomes more lethal. Oh, I didn't mean that. I meant blatantly violent. Oh, I mean…"

"You meant wait until I'm in the morgue or beaten to mush," said Margie.

"I didn't mean either of those," said Carolina. "I meant if we feel the crisis is beyond us. So far the agent of these depredations has made one person and one feline very sick."

"OK, Carolina," replied Margie. "I'm pacified. Let's get on with the plan."

"Does that mean we're all staying?" Carolina asked. She looked at each one until they agreed like a jury.

"So what's our plan?" said Carolina, "I brought you here to warn you, and to hear *your* ideas."

"Warn away," said Annie, who trusted almost everyone.

"Be careful with your food or anything you put in your mouth," said Carolina in her schoolmarm voice.

"We could each buy one of those metal containers of toothpaste. Poisoners can inject something in those plastic ones," said Dot, who'd just gotten her first can of toothpaste and didn't need to make a new investment.

"Yes," replied Carolina, "we put all kinds of food and drink and medicines in our bodies. Think about everything. Make sure the food comes fresh from the Courte's kitchen and pray we haven't insulted the cooking or serving staff too much."

"I think we're safe from antagonizing them since Lillian left. 'This is NOT food!' is no longer heard at our table," said Annie.

"How we all miss it too," replied Carolina. "Technically, the offer of tainted food could come from any of us here, of course."

"NOT!" or words to that effect came from the others. Then they looked soberly at the scones they were scarfing down.

"I agree," said Carolina. "None of us. We've proven our affection and loyalty to each other.

That's why I didn't ask Paula, although some of you might feel she's one of us now. She was not here to save the others last time. Anyway, the tainted food could come in an offhand way, very innocently, even at our 'weekly entertainments with wine glasses we leave on the table or from appetizers they leave out for us."

"I think I'll just go to jail again," said Margie. "I was safe and nobody there wanted me to be their bitc…"

"STOP!" they all shouted.

"Really, Margie, your language did get a bit corrupted there and you should stay out of jail if you can," advised Carolina.

"I didn't learn that language in jail. The women there stayed away from me, mostly because they thought I'd stabbed someone. I got cable there, and not even pay-for-view cable. Have you seen programs on Comedy Central like Colbert? They talk like that on cable now."

"Let's get back to cleaner things, like murder," said Dot.

Annie quickly said, "I think the fink is Mike. He never forgave us for criticizing him and for that trick you played Carolina, making us seem like long-lost relatives at his welcome home party."

"That was brilliant," said Rita.

"It just sort of happened," preened Carolina, which was way out of character for her, until she remembered that pride goeth before a fall.

"I think it's Mike too," said Dot.

"There's Frieda. She makes snide remarks to me but I stay away from her," said Margie.

"Let's keep an eye on everyone for strange behavior," said Carolina.

"Strange behavior here?" laughed Margie. "Let's take turns telling stories of strange behavior we saw just this week."

"Management put a new sign up on the concierge desk saying that no one is allowed behind the desk anymore. You have to ask the concierge if you want to go back to the offices and then he calls them to come out to make sure you don't wander around back there. Is that strange?" said Dot. "I'll bet that makes Mike angry."

"It may be out of the blue, like they do things here, but it's not strange. I hope they put those apartment keys in a locked case. I suggested that," said Carolina.

"I used to be strange but I don't wander around 24 hours a day looking for a quiet apartment anymore, and Apie doesn't stare at ghosts in our new apartment. It's noisy, though, from the elevator."

"Yes, Margie, you were strange," said someone trying not to be recognized in the group.

"I saw Frieda walking around writing down apartment numbers," said Rita.

They all looked with interest at her. "That's all," added Rita. "She was writing apartment down numbers. Of course, I couldn't ask why."

"Why not?" asked Dot.

"You know—manners."

"That's strange, since we have directories with our names, phone numbers, internet addresses and apartment numbers. Maybe she was writing down the apartments' locations in the building or something else," said Carolina.

"How about 'Miss Manners' at our table as a candidate?" asked Annie.

"She seems perfectly, boringly ordinary," said Margie who always looked frowzy and dumpy, and was somewhat jealous of Paula's neatness. "I wonder if she's a Stepford wife. That one could live in a clock."

"I saw Mr. Howard, the concierge, holding a 'help' button to call for emergencies. Only residents are supposed to have 'help' buttons. He put it in the breast pocket of his shirt," contributed Annie, trying to think of something she had seen that was odd somehow.

"It's understandable and not strange at all when you consider what happened to him," said Rita.

"Why not just use the fire alarm?" asked Margie, who had used that convenience to call for help in an emergency at another time.

"He might be in another room doing something or in the bathroom," said Dot, with criticism in her voice. "There isn't a fire alarm in every room."

"Well," said Carolina, winding the discussion down. "Now we're alert to our surroundings. Stay around other people when you can, outside of your locked apartments. Be careful where you talk. You know how people hear things around here."

"Let's leave like we came," said Annie. "That was fun."

"I'll clean up later," Carolina said to offers to help her clean up as her guests prepared to leave.

Margie was the last to leave. She had her head down on her arms as Carolina was by the door ushering her other friends out. Carolina lived in one of the more isolated corners of the Courte. She came back to the dining area to see Margie look up and smile. Carolina felt more resolve than ever, after seeing Margie's tragic, tired face trying to smile.

CHAPTER 14: GET OUT THE FIRE EXTINGUISHER

Life was interrupted again on the day they'd been told to save by the "Save the Date" cards. "The Day of Celebration" at the Courte was at hand. Carolina was with Annie when flyers announcing the program for the celebration day were distributed in their boxes. They did not read them until they got back to their rooms. If Carolina had read hers in the lobby, the Courte might have witnessed another incident of 'spontaneous human combustion' of the sort Dickens described in one of his books. Luckily, she was drinking a glass of water when she read it, sitting in her chair in her bedroom so she was able to put herself out at the first spark. Her words after reading it were, "Lord, no!" (both as prayer and profanity). This flyer was to lead to an unprecedented temporary change in Carolina, the likes of which the world had never seen before— or the world at the Courte anyway.

The flyer read:

ACTIVITIES FOR THE DAY OF CELEBRATION

11:00 A.M.-1:00 P.M.: *Bingo* in the library, board games in the game room, and *The Price Is Right* in the entertainment room (concurrently and simultaneously)

1:00-2:00 P.M.: Cat and Dog Show in the lobby (Register your pet at the concierge desk)

2:00-3:00 P.M: Walk in the Labyrinth in the Preserve, behind the parking lot (Special escorts will be provided for those with walkers or wheel chairs)

3:00-4:00 P.M.: Cocktails and hor d'oeuvres in the library.

4:00-5:00 P.M.: Polka Band in the entertainment room (Cocktails and wine served)

5:00-7:30 P.M.: Dinner as usual.

7:30-9:00 P.M.: Cocktails in the library, entertainment room and lobby. Dancing under the moonlight on the library patio and on the sundeck. Fortune teller available in the game room.

(Partners or escorts permitted, but not families. Sorry, there will not be enough room for the turnout of residents we expect.)

The very next day, Carolina passed the word around to her friends to meet at Margie's apartment at a certain time. She ignored their looks and requests for an explanation at her calling another secret group meeting. They all gathered on time with tremendous interest.

"No, no tea, Margie. This is business, serious business."

They looked at a frazzled Carolina whom they'd never seen before. Margie started to feel an anxiety attack coming on. Apie hid in the bedroom. Carolina got up in front of them like a teacher with an unruly class.

"Did you all see the program for the 'Day of Celebration'?"

"Yes, Carolina," they all replied in schoolgirl voices.

"We can't go, of course. It's too full of peril. We could all be knocked off. Count the ways. This could all be a plot of some sort," Carolina shuddered.

"Of course, we're going to go, Carolina. Don't be silly," said Annie. "Think of all of the fun we can have, and these days, fun doesn't come around for us so often anymore."

"It must be shock of some sort," said Dot to the other schoolgirls. "Did you hit your head, Carolina?"

Rita added with resolve, "I'm not sitting in my apartment all day!"

"I want to do it all," was Margie's desire. "Apie will win the pet contest. She's the most beautiful animal of all here. You all must be there to vote for her. Do you think a bow would help or would it be a distraction from her lines and colors?"

Carolina found a left over chair and, for the first time in her life other than at an odd funeral or two, cried.

Her friends looked at each other, appalled.

"Do you think someone slipped you something, Carolina?" Annie, who was never tentative, asked tentatively.

"Please don't cry," begged Margie.

Rita and Dot were dumbfounded and could say nothing. The world must be off its axis.

They all stared at Carolina and waited, as she dried her eyes on a tissue Margie had handed her. She took a deep breath.

"I'm sorry. I see I can't convince you. Maybe you could make some tea for us, Margie, please."

Carolina picked up the program that had fallen on the floor and studied it as Margie made tea and they drank it. Hardly anyone said a word. It was as if they'd seen the Dalai Lama punch someone on television. They thought Carolina should maybe see a doctor.

Finally, Carolina got up and said in her schoolteacher voice once again, "OK, here are the rules. I will be watching."

"Eat or drink only what is poured or you see being brought from the kitchen. Hold onto your plates and glasses. Do NOT set them down."

"Stay in pairs, at least in every activity. Maybe we should do everything in fives."

"Leave Apie in the apartment. She's been through enough."

"No dancing in the dark on the patio or sundeck."

"Avoid strangers, and Mike and Frieda and Paula and everyone else."

Carolina's voice got progressively louder. "Do not go into the labyrinth. It's dangerous for most of us, although it's not too far into the preserve and just across from our parking lot. You can still fall on roots or something. The volunteers are residents here. How do you know you can trust them not to push you into the pond or over the bridge railing? And they may be in worse shape than we are! It's a swamp over there. That's why the land was given as a preserve. No one wanted to build on it. At best, you can be bitten by ticks or mosquitoes with dengue fever or at worst attacked from behind the giant boulders beside the path like pioneers going through a mountain pass. We'll be falling like flies. STAY OUT OF THE WOODS!"

Carolina looked around to see who was shouting. She pulled herself together and said with quiet authority, "Do you understand?"

"Yes, Carolina," they all said soothingly as if they were talking to a lunatic, knowing all of the time that they were going to go into the labyrinth, and that Apolonia would be in the pet competition.

"Fine," replied Carolina, "I feel better now that you understand how we can remain relatively safe. Some of the activities seem entertaining and safe." She smiled tightly, then with more feeling. "We can even have some fun."

Apie came out of the bedroom and peeked out at the group. As it appeared there would be no vet or cat carriers today, she strutted to the middle of the group to give them all the special treat of her presence but surprisingly avoided her beloved Carolina.

CHAPTER 15: THE DREADED DAY OF CELEBRATION

The first floor was a wonderland of different colors. Apparently, there were no special colors that represented Courte life like there were for high school football teams. A rainbow of streamers and balloons abounded. The cheapest of paper decorations were on the tables—the ones that popped open like accordions to get more paper for your buck. The various printed parts of the decorations specifying the holiday had been cut off. Red, white and blue, and red and green decorations predominated. Carolina did think as she saw them that maybe Management had bid on a lot of "varied decorations" and this purchase had prompted the idea of a celebration of the Courte idea. Then they realized they had to spring for drinks and canapés and extra help herding residents. She wondered how that had gone over and who had cut apart the names of the holidays from the decorations in secret. But signs that simply said "Happy," "Happy," "Happy," "Happy," and "Merry" were everywhere in the public areas.

Carolina had come down early on the "special day" to check out possible hazards. She was a nervous wreck to begin with over this affair, although she wouldn't acknowledge it. How would she be later? This was the Carolina who'd been a rock during the late evacuation, during her whole life really. She collapsed just this once under the burden of keeping the five of them alive for the whole day—more like six, counting Apolonia. Thank heavens Apie would be safely locked up all day.

She checked out the game room. What could go wrong there? Games seemed like a sedate activity for the ladies, unless someone came in with a knife or something. There was no back door to that room to escape through. But the secret monster at the Courte did not seem to be a person of open violence, but of subterfuge, sure that he or she would walk away laughing after the depredations were complete. The singer part of the day would be safe too. All that the group had to do was sit and watch, and just be careful not to sit over electrical cords. She must warn them of that. The fortune teller, who was not a resident, was silly but probably not dispensing anything but lies and happy predictions.

Eating and drinking were the only activities Carolina had to monitor for all of them. Preventing a poisoning was tricky in a crowd.

And no walking in the woods!

Carolina checked out the second floor sundeck too. The railing around it was pretty high and the group would only go up there together, if at all, she would insist on that. She breathed a sigh of relief. All would be well. She'd controlled classes of rowdy teenage boys in the past. Surely herding four elderly ladies would be a piece of cake. Today was really the safe day as far as she was concerned because they'd be together (she told herself). The rest of the time was dangerous when they were each at ease and alone. Carolina began to be convinced that she could be "Happy," "Happy," "Happy," "Happy," and "Merry" along with everyone else. She went back to her apartment to get ready for the fun day.

They all met at Margie's apartment at a quarter of 11:00 to leave together, since Carolina wanted to be sure Apie was locked in the apartment securely as they left.

"Remember," (she almost said 'girls'), stay together and go to the bathroom in pairs only—at the very least, in pairs."

The other women had decided to humor Carolina this one day only, and get her professional help if her personality change continued.

The Courte was filled with *oohs!* and *ahs!* over the decorations. The staff all dressed in black slacks and white shirts, not the same—except for the colors. Board games were set up in the game room, Bingo was being prepared in the library complete with Dollar Store prizes, and something was being set up in the entertainment/video room. This set-up was making Carolina breathe easier. It all seemed so familiar, like one's living room.

Then came the first sign that things might not go so well. Rita set off for the board game room,

Dot for Bingo, Annie to talk with friends on the front veranda and Margie wandered into the entertainment room to see what was being planned there. The place began to flood with people. Carolina looked bewildered as if her toddlers had wandered off by themselves and she didn't know how to corral them or which to follow first. People began to talk to her. Most of the sewing circle surrounded her.

"Did you bring your aunt's sampler down?" asked Gretchen.

"Uh, no, sorry," said a distracted Carolina.

"We're going to knit and crochet in the library as usual and ignore the Bingo," sniffed Enid.

Numbers were being called loudly from the open library, but old Florence said, "What Bingo?" Carolina, even in her distress, admired their ability to concentrate.

"I'm thinking about more food for my family today," said Gretchen.

"Food?" asked Carolina. "You mean specialty items from a catalog or something?"

"No, I mean yams and eggplant and squash and the like."

"I didn't imagine they were so poor from what you'd said about them."

"Poor? No, I meant knitting. Fruit isn't enough. I'll stuff the vegetables with polyester foam later. They'll love them! When I'm there, I wear black dresses with simple pearls since I don't want to take away the only time they can shine. Paula wants to buy our work but said she wants 'plainer' stuff. What can she mean by that? I can knit pearls in thread, you know, and pins and other jewelry into the clothes. Then I can glue giant glass jewels on them."

The other sewing circle members looked at Gretchen with reverence. They left to set up their chairs in the middle of the Bingo people. Carolina started to wonder again if Gretchen was as oblivious to other people's reactions as she'd originally thought.

No food or drink was yet being served. Carolina decided she could just sit in the lobby and watch the doors to the rooms where her four friends were, in case Frieda came out to fight or something.

Suddenly everyone heard, "You're the winner!"

Carolina, as well as many of the people in the other rooms, went to the entertainment room where they were playing The Price Is Right to see slides projected on the wall of pictures of prizes— refrigerators, blenders, heart-shaped bathtubs and medical appliances. Margie was apparently on a roll and clapped her hands whenever she guessed the price of a projected prize right. The other two contestants were not even close. Everyone wanted Margie to guess which strand of pearls was real just from looking at the fuzzy slides on the wall. They all wanted to be part of that! There was a mob scene as the crowd tried to enter the room at the same time.

"Stop! Stop!" said Loretta. "We want to play too."

Carolina found herself in the middle of the mob, many with walkers. She saw Annie behind her with hers, and Rita in the back and Dot being squeezed in the doorway. Margie, the apparent winner, was disappointed at having her total victory and future winnings (the fake pearls) postponed if not taken away from her as usual. Angie tried to stem the tide of the approaching people by saying there wasn't enough room. The show was over! Margie got down from the little stage area and found her way to the poker room door, where there was an exit, to go to her room and cry. Loss was her Karma it appeared. In horror, Carolina saw Frieda approaching the unsuspecting Margie from the poker room to stare her in the face. Margie panicked and only appeared to want to get out of the room.

Frieda pointed her arm and index finger at Margie like the humanoid pods in the *Invasion of the Body Snatchers* and shouted to one and all, "Look at her! She caused this mess and riot. She's a Communist! Look at her in those awful clothes. She's a menace and an eyesore!"

Margie was trapped and Carolina couldn't get to her. Margie looked for a window or something to jump out of seemingly, even though it was the ground floor. Suddenly, the concierge, Mr. Howard, entered the room with a whistle that he blew which sounded like something between a foghorn and a piercing scream.

All noise and movement stopped. He had entered by the poker room door, told Frieda to leave, and escorted the frightened Margie out of the door to the elevator. After Margie disappeared in it, the room broke out in applause and shouts of "Hooray for Mr. Howard!" Angie turned on some Mexican fiesta music and most of the crowd started to dance in their walkers or without them. Some discussed dedicating a shrine to Mr. Howard, the hero of the hour. Carolina tried to point her other dinner friends to a meeting in the hallway, but all were caught up in the music and dancing, except for Dot who harrumphed at her predicament and just wanted to get out of there. The Price Is Right was not right for her.

Mike, who apparently had started celebrating the night before, took the Dollar Store prizes and threw them around the room. Pandemonium reigned as Mr. Howard blew his whistle again, and all of the Courte's workers ushered the people out of the entertainment room to the patio and halls and veranda.

Carolina would have fallen had she not been supported by the crowd around her. *If this was the start of the day, what could be next?* she wondered. *This must be how Margie feels most of the time*, was a fleeting thought in her mind.

Carolina soon found out what was next. She heard barking from several places on the floor. She heard a cat hissing and growling too.

The dogs were on leashes, but one had pulled away from its guardian and was chasing Mrs. Bloomfield's cat who ran up the curtains in the library.

Mrs. Bloomfield yelled, "Get Dolly down please! Close the library door to the outside. I'll never get her back if she runs away. Please, please! She's my best friend."

Mr. Howard came in with his whistle, which only upset the animals more, the high notes driving the dogs wild. Then to Carolina's horror, the elevator opened to show Margie standing there with Apolonia.

The first floor was chaos. Margie who was coming toward the lobby, was pushed back into the elevator by people crowding in, isolating her from Carolina who wanted to save Margie and her cat. Carolina managed to push her way into the elevator since the door was being held open by people trying to get in. Apie escaped from Margie's arms and was running between people's legs. They were all screaming. Carolina made a grab under Mrs. Mealey's skirts and caught the beautiful calico cat in her arms just in time for her and Apie to get out on Margie's floor. The people on the elevator pushed Margie out too, whether inadvertently or with malice one couldn't say.

The three headed for Margie's apartment and escaped inside.

"Why, Margie, why did you ever bring Apolonia to the pet show?" asked Carolina, panting. "It was not fun for her and, after your encounter with Frieda, I thought you'd want to be in your apartment for the rest of the day, surely."

Apie, by this time, was under Margie's bed and really mad. Margie would have a long time to wait before she forgave her!

"I promised to be there and they put Apie on the ballot. I know my Apolonia is the prettiest and best cat here and want her to get appreciation for it. I'm sorry. I'm so sorry, Apie," Margie yelled to the bedroom. Carolina and Margie collapsed, both too overwhelmed to cry.

"What about the labyrinth?" asked Margie.

"What about it?" said Carolina. "We're not going. Not you, not me, and not Annie and not Dot and not Rita. They promised."

"But they are going, Carolina!" replied Margie, frightened. "We signed up. The others may be on their way now."

Carolina was shell shocked. "But they promised. You promised!"

"We just promised to placate you, Carolina. You were being so bossy. We thought you'd lighten up on the day of fun."

Carolina suddenly stood. "We have to go. We can walk better, but Annie and Dot need help with their walkers. They're going into the woods! We must save them."

Margie and Carolina got themselves together enough to leave the apartment and venture outside. Luckily, both of them were already wearing sensible shoes so they didn't have to change.

The so-called "hiking" group had disappeared on the trail, but they could be heard laughing in the distance. The labyrinth was a circle of stones in a fenced-off area of the woods. The steady walkers among them had taken the hiking trail;

the ones with walkers and wheel chairs took a service road.

The trail was quicker, so Carolina and Margie opted for that. "Look at those roots and little rocks; anyone could slip on them. What was Management thinking?" asked Carolina. "Look at the trees. Anybody could be behind any one of them, picking off the stragglers."

"We're the stragglers," Margie pointed out, matter of factly. "I think the others stayed pretty much together so they'll be OK," said Margie, pleased to be the one in the reasonable role for a change.

They arrived at the fencing with the door wide open, just in time to see their friends sitting on stone benches around the circled path while a preserve representative in the middle explained the historical meaning of the labyrinth, which he said was supposed to have a calming effect on people.

"What about those hex signs everywhere?" asked Annie.

"Well, groups of kids are known to come into the preserve at night and party. They somehow get the locked gate open or jump over the fence."

"What about that printed sign up there that says 'no devil worshippers allowed'?" Margie asked.

"Oh, that's a joke," said the representative with a laugh, "although some groups are known to come to the labyrinth at night and...worship here." The ranger, or whatever he was, looked embarrassed. "The labyrinth is a cultural and educational monument. Nothing else."

"Who knew we had devil worshippers so close to home?" said an anonymous voice from the group.

"Who says the worshippers aren't from the Courte?" a hollow-sounding, muffled voice from the back of the group said knowingly.

They all participated in a group shudder and were silent.

"Time to go back," said the concierge leading the outing. "More fun is waiting."

Carolina wanted to run for the highway in the distance to hitchhike her way as far away from this place as she could get, but instead gathered her friends and their volunteer escorts and said they could all go back together by the service road.

The walk back was hard and long with many of the tired residents needing help. They passed a few boulders and the pond safely, until they made it the short way to the Courte. Carolina again breathed with relief, a sure sign that more trouble was at hand.

"No blood sacrifices today," remarked Dot.

Carolina gave her an offended look.

The worst remained. They came back to be greeted by several trays full of hor d'oeuvres and an open bar.

"Remember," hissed Carolina, "one plate and one drink in your hands at all times! Do not ever set them down. You know the possible consequences if you do!"

"Yes, mother," Annie answered with sarcasm.

Carolina surprised them all by getting in front of everyone so that she could order a scotch and soda. She sat down in the library to watch her friends and to grab anything they might set down if they were distracted.

The hour was a horror. Annie schmoozed, setting everything on her walker shelf and visiting different groups. Plate after plate was thrown by Carolina into the garbage in case it had been tampered with. Margie and Dot behaved, seeing Carolina's eyes upon them. Rita got a verbal warning, Carolina watching her plate and drink carefully. But what of Carolina's own drinks when she was watching the others' food and drink?

Carolina wound up ordering two more drinks for herself until she got "the look" from Angie who was serving and suggested that enough was enough. One would have been plenty, her face said.

Entertainment hour was then called. People followed each other into the room to hear "Murray Finklestein and his Genuine Polka Band."

Carolina thought she might lie down until dinner and miss the band which would shake the walls of the entertainment room where there were never enough chairs for everyone. She was leaving, astonishing everyone with her offish manner, when she saw the new horror. Carts of food piled with leftovers were set out for self-service on the floor, as well as bottles of wine. *Half of the Courte could be poisoned* was Carolina's thought. But the bulwark that had been

Carolina did not care anymore. She had to lie down even if the whole place disappeared without her there to save them. So Mike, Frieda and Paula, and any other possible murderer mingled among them with impunity. Carolina, the mighty, had struck out, had abandoned her post.

The residents and workers consumed the canapés and wine with no ill effects, except headaches and indigestion. The residents gobbled everything in preparation for their four-course dinners coming up. All of that junk food seemed only to whet their appetites for fried food, cream sauces and fancy desserts.

At dinner, the dining room was a lively and happy place, everyone talking about the excitement of the day and the amusements to come. The usual six gathered at their table in the left far corner.

"I'm deaf from the music," Rita was saying. "My head was pounding in that room."

"I love polkas," said Margie, humming the Julida Polka. "I would have named my daughter Julida if I'd had one, although it wasn't nice of the girl in the song to only want her boyfriend's money. Do you think it would have bothered my daughter to be named after her?"

"I did think the lyrics of some of the songs were odd," said Dot, ignoring Margie's question about her mythical daughter. "They sang something about a boyfriend watching his girlfriend wash her feet."

"Folk music, you see..." lectured Margie.

They all looked at Carolina since she knew so much about everything. But there were no lectures from the wilted woman who looked like she hardly knew what a fork was for tonight.

"Tired?" asked Paula.

"Yes, thank you," was Carolina's feeble response. She needed a summer in the Caribbean and not just an hour of rest on her couch. Besides, she had what she wouldn't acknowledge was a hangover.

The others went on speaking with eagerness around her.

"What are you all going to do tonight?" asked Annie.

"It's all over, it's all over" was the only thing Carolina could say.

The others looked past her as they would have if someone was slightly drunk at their table but with sadness in their eyes. Not their Carolina.

"I want to dance. I used to dress up to the nines and go out dancing every Saturday night with my honey," reminisced Rita.

"Oh, you had a boyfriend?" asked Margie, not having been called pet names much in her marriage.

Rita was ready to get into a fighting match with Margie until she realized that Margie was not being insulting. "My honey was my *husband*."

"Oh, sorry, honest." Margie was born apologizing.

"That's OK. I did have some boyfriends before and after my marriage. That's natural, isn't it?" said Rita.

As natural as a fish with a bicycle, I suppose, Margie almost said, but remembered that one of her heroes, Gloria Steinem, who'd made that famous statement in better form, had eventually married and very happily too.

Rita then said, "I'm going to get my fortune told. I hope they have a good teller and not just some staff member dressed up like a Gypsy in the movies."

Everyone knew what Rita wanted to know. The fortune teller would have an easy reading with her.

Margie thought the reading might not be for her; she knew the news would be bad if the fortune teller was any good.

Dot said, "I might take my chance. It will be amusing. I have no skeletons in my closet to be afraid of. What about you, Paula?"

The others were thinking they'd like to know about private Paula too. Maybe there was nothing to know.

Paula looked around with some fear in her eyes. "I had a bad experience with one once. She saw my hotel key number when I went to pay her and my room was robbed that evening."

The others wondered if that was the genuine reason for her fear. It made sense though.

"You don't have to worry about tonight. You won't need your purse. This fortune teller is free," said Annie. "Everyone should go. We don't often get free things here."

"It seems against the laws of God," Paula said, defending herself. "I mean, fortune telling—not getting free things."

"Only if you believe in fortune telling," said Carolina quietly, "although some people are given special gifts."

"You always know who the robbers and killers are, Carolina. Maybe you should read fortunes," positive Annie said to her best friend.

"I only use logic, like Sherlock Holmes."

"Music and dancing tonight too. What a wonderful day. It would be perfect if only Floyd could play the piano too. I feel like I'm 16 years old again." Annie was in heaven.

Margie looked like her regular unhappy self and said, "Well, Apie almost got trampled and is mad at me and I missed out on the fake pearls and then that Frieda episode today. And Carolina seems beat."

"Listen," said Dot.

Just then, the concierge on duty was making an announcement to the room. These announcements were usually about illnesses or something bad or a car parked illegally. But he was saying, "The winner of our contest for Best Pet in Show at the Courte was won by a cat named Apolonia. Her owner may pick up her ribbon at the concierge desk at any time. Congratulations"

Margie was thrilled, stating, "Oh, my! Apolonia will be so proud! I didn't think they got around to voting with all of that commotion going on. I guess today was not so bad after all." (Carolina smiled inside knowing that she'd been one of the only ones to fill out a voting form and hand it in at the desk. She had a feeling that the count that day with all of those distractions that occurred was Apolonia (1 vote) and others (none).

"Today was great for me except my food and drinks kept disappearing during our cocktail time. But I'm happy," sighed Annie who was usually happy anyway.

"You should not have left your food unattended. Probably someone from the Courte cleaned up efficiently." Carolina thought her nose might grow after saying that, and she'd have to pray about it too. The day was not just bad for her, it was unholy. And she, a person who'd been taught never to waste, had discarded all of that food too, even it was to keep her friend Annie safe.

They finished their dinners and left to get ready for the evening of dancing and socializing. They left the dining room and walked down the hall (taking a long time because of Annie's popularity). They passed the game room that was made up with cardboard around the door to look like a fortune teller's tent. The tables inside were set up, one for waiting and one for the telling. The teller was dressed in the usual peasant dress with a bandana in her hair. An assistant was helping to set up the room. The assistant was probably part of the act sent around to pick up information for the teller to use. Maybe the staff had told her things about them.

"At least the Courte has hired a real fortune teller," said Rita.

"Well, a paid one, anyway," replied Dot. "You don't know if she has real psychic powers."

The group broke up to rest or primp or read mail or talk to other people for the next hour. They were to meet, all six of them, in the library at 7:15.

Carolina crept down at that time on this endless day, using her cane for real in her weakened state. They met in the lobby but there was no room to sit down. They drifted off to the fortune teller's area to sit in the poker room next to it. The fortune teller's assistant was handing out time cards and suspiciously "mingling." The six women got tickets in succession. No one wanted to opt out of the group and disappoint the others. Their appointments started at 8:00. They could come in at 7:45 to sit down in the teller's room to keep the flow steady into the tent.

Music started in the library, pumped through the sound system to the lobby and the entertainment room. Tea and coffee were available with ice in the library.

"One glass only," warned Carolina, as they went in the library, "or let me hold it for you. I won't be dancing." Carolina found a seat. Her eyes closed in spite of herself. She violated a reportable Courte rule: No sleeping in the library. Usually only violators who lay down on the couches or snored were reported and sent to their rooms like naughty children. Loretta, the control freak of the Courte, objected to sleepers in the library so strongly that she wanted to have a fine imposed on them. But she was considered a radical.

Annie melted into the biggest group, drinking her iced tea, oblivious to anything someone might put into her drink. The poisoner had better not be after her or she was a goner.

Dot sat in her cheerful chic vintage night clubby hat in black with a shiny 1920's pattern. She liked the big band music being played.

Rita has found a partner and was off on the library patio dancing with a nice man whose wife had cheerfully volunteered him so she could talk in peace. Rita was in heaven, except for the man not being eligible. Her happiness was eclipsed a bit by Beverly in her gold high heels introducing her new boyfriend, a doctor.

Margie went to visit Apie, waiting for the reading time.

Paula was here and there mostly around the first floor. Her companion, until Paula could ditch her, was Frieda, who seemed to be lecturing her on how could she stand that table with that Margie there, "Did you see her shoes? Those same sandals she wears day and night..."

The time came. The other five surrounded Carolina who was called awake by her friends looming over her. *Were they dead and accusing her?* was her first guilty thought to go along with her bad dreams.

"Time to go to the 'room,' Carolina."

She got up and went with them as if to the guillotine. She felt a sense of oppression. Maybe it was just that odd headache she had and the queasiness.

The assistant was seating them at the waiting table until each was ready to go under the black blanket hanging over the smaller fortune teller's table to give the client a feeling of privacy, although everyone could hear what was said.

"So shall I die on the Blessed Isle?" they heard a drunken voice asking.

"No! Yes, if you are a good boy and remove your hand!" A slap was heard and soon a man was escorted out of the room and put on an elevator.

The assistant called Rita to the sacred area under the blanket.

"Oh, it's dark in here."

"Shhh! Shhhh!" said the fortune teller. "Do not disturb Madame Tsarita," she said in her overdone Bela Lugosi accent. "My mind must be free to sense, to KNOW! I see you are a lover of beautiful clothes, jewelry, dancing, maybe?"

"How did you know? You are wonderful!"

"You will meet a tall man with gray hair, well dressed. He will give you gifts. You will travel. You will die within a week of each other so that you will never be lonely again. But that time of parting will not come for a long, long time. That is all."

"But who is…."

"NEXT!"

Rita left reluctantly, but with her heart soaring. Paula got up to say, "Take my time. I don't mind."

"No" said the fortune teller. "I said NEXT! Do not upset Madame Tsarita."

Dot, who was next, made her way to the main tent.

"Ah. Put your hand over the candle. Is it shaking? I see. I see. You will never take up drugs again. You are free!"

Dot left embarrassed while the others seemed annoyed that their friend should be treated that way. Dot's private problem with prescription drugs had been in the past.

Then it was Annie's turn.

"You have known true love. People like you. You are the head of a strong family."

"Is that all?" Annie's disappointed voice was heard saying by the others.

"Enjoy your life. It has some excitement now. What more do you want? NEXT!"

"Oh, and don't get involved with a slick man who plays the piano."

Annie passed Margie going in. Margie hoped the fortune teller would tell her good, even if sort of boring, things. She sat down. The teller had been looking at her clothes and shoes as she sat before the curtain was lowered.

"Your life changed. You now attract drama to yourself. You should dress better and people will like you more. Forget your past. He was bad news. He is happy; you are not. Do something about yourself."

"What?"

"How do I know? Lose weight, get a personal dresser. NEXT!"

Paula's turn was next. Paula hesitated, so the fortune teller got out of her "tent" and stood up. Suddenly, Paula pointed to her and said. "I know her! I know her! She's evil. She's here to do harm. I left my home to get away from her. She follows me in disguises!"

Staff members, hearing the commotion, rushed in.

Paula quietly said, "I just don't want to have my fortune told." She would never talk again about what had really happened. The others felt like they had imagined the whole incident.

The fortune teller's assistant said, "It's a legal requirement that Madame Tsarita take her break. We will start with the next group in 15 minutes."

Carolina and the rest were ushered out. Music was still playing in the library. Only Rita wanted to go see the dancing but her partner was gone. "Let's go up to see what's going on at the sundeck," she proposed. She didn't want to go back to her apartment yet.

They all turned to the elevator and filed in, going to the sunroof floor. They walked in silence.

Lights in paper lanterns surrounded the deck. Fake candles were on the tables. The same music as downstairs was being piped in. The night was beautiful as they filed through the door. They saw some groups around the floor, a few couples were dancing. They went to talk to Ike and Joyce, his girlfriend, who were with Milton and Maxine. Paula drifted away. Margie moved to be near

Carolina when she saw Mike with his head down on a table. Annie moved to a dark corner to look out over the railing to see the moon. She was getting tired, the fortune teller had made her a bit melancholy, unusual for her. They were here now to calm down after the hectic day.

"Well, Ike, did you get your fortune told?" asked Rita.

"Yes, although I think she was a plant," he said suspiciously.

His new girlfriend cut in before they could ask, "She told him he'd be married twice and the second very soon," she laughed.

Ike countered. "And she told Joyce here that she'd be married soon too and would she be sorry!"

"So which statement are you mad about?" asked Dot.

"Help! Help!" a voice interrupted them.

They looked around to see Annie holding onto the railing. There had been a small gap between it and the wall on the corner where her hand was stuck. They all rushed over to grab Annie and help her sit down.

"Someone pushed me!" she managed to say.

They looked around to see Mike raise his head from the table behind them. Frieda was just coming in the door. But how long had she really been on the roof? That was an old ploy, to pretend you're just coming in. But the perpetrator could have backed out of the dark shadows on the roof and be mingling with them now too.

"Should we call a doctor or the police for you, Annie?" asked Carolina.

"No, no, I'm OK. Don't call anybody. Maybe I was just tired and fell asleep looking over the railing and my hand missed the railing. It was so dark and pretty to look out on this corner." She sounded more disappointed that she had been interrupted than anything else.

With nothing to be done, they all headed for the door and their apartments, saying good-night as each drifted off toward their destinations. Carolina followed Annie in her walker and made sure she was comfortable inside before she left. Annie said she was going to bed. As Carolina left, Annie said, "Someone did push me, Carolina."

Carolina went toward her apartment, walking down her long hall with nervousness. She got in her apartment to thank God that they'd all survived the 'Day of Celebration' when her phone rang.

"It's Margie. Apie was standing outside my door when I came home. How did she get out? I don't think maintenance was in here tonight. I'm scared."

"I'll be right down," said Carolina, wondering if this night would ever be over.

"Don't. I checked. Nobody is here. The chain is up."

"Watch what you eat and drink. You know the drill."

"I will. I'll call you if I need you. Good night, Carolina."

Carolina went to bed saying bitterly to herself that all good things must come to an end. (And all bad things too. Carolina would be her old self when she awoke in the morning as if her fairy godmother had removed a bad spell.)

CHAPTER 16: *CAMILLE* AMONG THE FLESHPOTS

The day came for *Camille*, Annie's favorite movie. All five of the friends were there, Paula having made some excuse not to come. They sat in the front row of three long rows set up lengthwise in the library. About nine women and one man showed up for the viewing. Everyone in the dining room knew of Annie's love for Greta Garbo and the story of the party girl who'd found true love too late.

"She' so beautiful. My mother loved her too," said Annie, who sat between Carolina and Dot.

"Of course, the movie has stood the test of time," said Rita who sat next to Dot.

Stragglers came in, acknowledging Annie and her friends.

"We came because we heard you liked it so much, Annie," a few of them said.

"Speak for yourselves; I always loved Garbo myself," said Gretchen.

"I come to all of the movies," said Carla.

"We'll all enjoy it together," said Carolina, calming egos.

Everyone settled down. It was past 8 P.M., the time the movie should have started. The seats were close together. Walkers were set at the ends of the rows of chairs. Some residents wanted to rest their feet on their walkers, but there was no room tonight to move chairs out of the way. The front row people usually could rest their feet, but not tonight. There was excitement in the air, spreading out from the first row.

The whole floor was noisy tonight. More people than usual were meeting in the library, and the lobby was crowded with people coming and going and meeting up with visitors. There was unusual life in the old folks' home tonight—a night people would talk about for years.

The concierge on duty was late coming into put the rented film in the DVD.

"They might have mixed the films up again, Annie. You might not see it," someone said.

"No, we will. I saw the afternoon show," said another.

"That's cheating," said Dot, to whoever had said that.

The concierge was busy helping a resident open her mailbox, since she'd inserted the wrong key which had then gotten stuck. The mailboxes were in a little room across from the elevator, which is why the concierge did not stop the well-built young man who was wearing some sort of stretchy tuxedo with a bow tie and carrying a strange box.

"Where's the Camille party?" he asked several residents in the lobby, loudly. They all pointed to the library. The man entered the library and took in the sight before him, probably thinking that

some days you really earn your money. He
shrugged his shoulders. The lights were still on.
He walked to the front of the group. They all
looked up at him curiously. Some of the people
from the lobby came over to look through the
doorway.

The young man made movements with the box
that he'd placed on the floor. It began to play loud
music with a loud beat. The group of residents sat
in their chairs as if paralyzed.

"This space is too rather small, but the closer
the better, right girls?" shouted the young man
over the music.

He pulled out a paper and yelled, "Where are
Camille, Carolina, Margie, Annie, Dot and Rita? I
presume Camille is the bride and the rest of you
are bridesmaids? What's the fella doing here?" He
gestured to Milton, the lone man in the front row.
"You're welcome to watch too, buddy."

Milton, who'd taken a break from doing his
models, looked confused, then turned an
apoplectic red. He started to say something when
the young man began gyrating his hips and
leering. The next thing the young man did was
pull off his suit in one quick movement and stood
there in a black thong and white bow tie attached
by a band around his neck. The residents could all
see his sparse underwear in front. He started to
bend over Carolina, putting his hands on her
shoulders.

More people collected around the door and
some came inside to look. They separated when

they heard a man's voice screaming at them to let him pass.

The concierge came bursting into the room. One old man was holding a cane in the air, trying to get out of his row of seats, and threatening to attack someone.

They all turned and looked at the now screaming concierge, who was standing there like an avenging angel. "Miss Pennsbury, what are you doing?" he cried as the scantily clad young man bent over Carolina. "You *know* this is not allowed here!"

"And you," he screeched, pointing his arm extended to the man in the bow tie. "Get out or I'll call the police! Don't you know this is an old age home?" (Beverly, who'd come in to see what was happening, made a note to report the concierge to Management for *that* remark.)

The young man stood up from attending to Carolina, confused, and said, "I'm here to do a party, for a girl named Camille, and her bridesmaids Margie, Carolina, Annie, Dot, and Rita." He seemed proud that he'd remembered the names from memory. "I was paid by cash in the mail. I guess the person didn't want credit for his special surprise."

"Get out! Get out! Get out!" the concierge screamed.

The young man picked up his costume and his boom box that was still playing, and left as fast as he could, yelling "No Refunds!" to whoever could hear as he exited. The people watching him moved faster than they had in years to let him pass. Everyone in the lobby and the library looked like they'd seen aliens landing, as the man ran out, wearing nothing but a thong and a bow tie and numerous tattoos over his muscular body. Time had finally stopped at the Courte.

The young man ran to his car which had his business name, "Larry's Stripping" painted on the sides.

Vern, a resident who had been a bailiff and who had an obsession about the parking lot, met Larry outside his car. "Is this your car? I'm going to call the police. You have no right to park in resident spaces!"

The stripper stopped when he heard the old man yelling at him, but brushed him aside to get in his car. He pulled out, almost hitting Vern.

Inside, pandemonium ruled. One heard: "Carolina, who ordered a stripper?"

"Margie!"

"I'm not surprised at that!"

"Who's getting married?"

"I thought Camille was a movie."

"I thought Dot had more class."

"That's ridiculous! The stripper would have been wearing a hat if Dot had hired him."

"I'm taking my parents out of here tomorrow!"

The concierge, Mr. Howard, told Carolina, Annie, Margie, Dot and Rita to meet him behind the concierge desk. He put the movie in the DVD player and turned out the lights, hoping the majority would calm down and stay to watch the movie. However, the rest of the moviegoers followed him and the "wedding party" out of the room. They all filed out the door in a heap, many with walkers and canes, shouting threats of violence to each other if they didn't get out of the way. None of them wanted to miss the show—and not the one now playing in the DVD.

The miscreants passed everyone in the lobby as they were herded behind the concierge desk. Carolina saw Frieda smirking at them, and Mike was doubled up in laughter. The other onlookers looked shocked or ready to organize a vigilante group if requested.

"Who's getting married?" they heard Loretta's friend Hazel shouting, although it was a timid shout.

Vern came in from his parking-lot run-in with the stripper, shouting, "I hear you started this, Carolina. You know visitors are not supposed to park in resident spaces. The spaces are clearly marked. Everyone thinks they're privileged characters! You better tell your 'friend' he's in trouble. I got his license number. Who's 'Larry's Stripping' anyway? Larry's in big trouble and so are you! You'll probably get a warning letter from Management! Larry had better not come back."

The five women stood around the concierge's chair, now protected from group violence by the large hardwood concierge counter, but they could still be seen.

The avenging angel, otherwise known as the concierge spoke, "Ladies, ladies, you can't behave like this here. There are rules about guests and there is a dress code. What you did was very wrong. I'm going to have to report you."

"Enough!" said Carolina in a raised voice so everyone could hear her. She usually prided herself on a composed demeanor in emergencies, but this was too much. "We don't know any more about this than you do. We went to see the movie."

Suddenly, Dot, of all people who typically grumbled but never yelled, lost her temper. "Did you hear that, people? We don't know any more about it than you do! Or maybe one of you does. It was a set-up. One or more of you probably did it!"

Margie, who was used to being bullied, put her hand on Dot's arm, telling her it was all right. They would all be OK.

"What are you talking about?" replied Dot. "Of course we're OK!" Then, "Why did the man say you paid him, Carolina?"

"He didn't." said Carolina.

"Why didn't you bring him to your apartment and not expose us to your filth?" demanded Frieda.

"Let's leave," said Carolina to her friends. "Let's go to my apartment." She said to the concierge as they left, "Report away and don't patronize us again!"

They left, walking to the elevator past the movie room.

"Can I go in and watch the movie now?" asked Annie plaintively. The movie was still playing to an empty room.

"I don't think you should," advised Carolina. "We can buy it or rent it another day. We should talk about this incident. People will bother you if you go in there."

They got to Carolina's apartment, this time sitting on her couch and armchairs in her sitting/guest room.

"Who wants coffee, tea or sherry?" she asked.

"I can get some whiskey from my apartment if you want a real drink," said Rita.

"I have some hard liquor too," said Carolina.

"We heard you make it in your bathtub," laughed Margie.

"Just put whatever it is on the table and we can put it in our tea or coffee," said Annie. "I want to forget I'm missing the movie. I wonder what's happening now."

Carolina went to heat the water for tea and put coffee in her coffee maker.

"I want to forget that everyone hates us now," said Margie.

"Everyone doesn't hate us," said Rita with impatience.

They made themselves comfortable. Carolina came in with a tray of coffee, tea, cream, sugar and some bottles. She put it down and brought in another tray with Spode cups and silver spoons. She poured the coffee and tea and they handed around the bottles to whoever wanted to add liquor.

Carolina got up to get some crackers, but the others told her to sit.

"I'll get the box, you might need something to eat with your drinks," she said.

They all sat down together.

"As long as we have each other as friends, I guess we'll be OK," said Margie, relaxing.

"People like me. They always like me wherever I am," said Annie.

Carolina said, "Whom do you think did this to us and why?"

"You mean it's started again?" asked Margie, getting tense again.

"Of course," said Dot, "unless one of us ordered the stripper."

"Well, this didn't seem to have the viciousness of the other attacks. But I could be wrong," said Carolina thoughtfully. *It was more like a Puck trick than an Iago hateful, deadly scheme*, she thought to herself.

Suddenly, Margie began to giggle, followed by Annie and then Rita, then Dot and finally Carolina.

The uncontrollable laughter could have been the effect of the night or just the realization of the ridiculous trick. They hadn't even drunk much, especially Dot who'd had a prescription drug problem in the past and usually didn't drink anything with caffeine even.

Margie said she was tired. She got up to take her cup to the kitchen.

"Oh, leave it," said Carolina. "Does anyone want more?"

"No, we're all tired," said Annie. "I guess the movie is over."

"Yes, forget it," said Dot.

"Does anyone have any ideas about who did this tonight?" asked Carolina again.

"No," they all answered.

"Do you?" asked Margie.

"Well, yes, but I have to think about it since it doesn't make sense."

They got up to leave, this time leaving Carolina's apartment all together. They had had their fill of playing cloak and dagger for a while.

The next day, all six of the women sat in their regular places at the dining table. Five of them had had to face snickers and humphs and various other sounds from the people in the dining room and on the way down.

"Where are our 'A's for adulterers?" asked Margie.

"Don't worry, they're there in their minds," said Rita.

But not imprinted on our chests like the Reverend Arthur Dimmesdale. He was guilty, we are not. We must face contumely as it says. Where is that from? Carolina asked herself. When she forgot references, times were bad.

"We have friends," said Annie. "I have lots," she protested defensively.

"Really? Go up and talk to them after dinner. Politicians can pull off scandal but not old women in a retirement home," said Dot with cynicism.

"Things like this should mean nothing in these liberal days. We're not in high school. I mean, you all must have urges," said Paula, distastefully, but showing that she did not reject them as companions.

"We didn't plan it," said Margie.

"Oh, I'm sure you didn't," Paula assured them unconvincingly.

"Maybe I should move now," said Margie. "Management would probably be happy to see me go and not keep me to my lease."

"Ha!" said Annie. "Fat chance. There are only two ways of getting out of that lease—pay it in full or..." She symbolically cut her throat with a movement of her hand.

People at nearby tables nodded their heads, indicating that the crew in the corner were living up to their bloodthirsty and profligate reputation.

"Stop that, Annie!" barked Rita. "We must all be on our most proper behavior, above reproach."

"Paula likes us still," said Annie.

They all looked at Paula.

"Sorry I couldn't be with you last night. I was out buying some special food. The taxi brought me back just when you all were leaving from the lobby."

"Very convenient," mumbled Dot to herself.

"We appreciate your associating with us now," said Rita primly.

"This does not seem to be our year for high popularity ratings," said Carolina.

"They promised us undying adoration and gratitude for finding that killer a few months ago," said Margie. "The transience of fame is almost universally acknowledged by those who have enjoyed it at one time."

"You sound like Mary in *Pride and Prejudice*," said Carolina.

"Who's Mary?" asked Annie.

"Elizabeth's pompous sister," said Carolina. "Nevermind; I'm not at my best tonight."

The servers came out late, making their table wait. Apparently, the staff were going to make them suffer for what they considered the table's mean treatment of their friend Nello, the night concierge, the night before.

"We will turn things around again," said Carolina. "We have been through something like this before and overcame it."

Everyone but Annie looked skeptical.

Three women came over to their table, looking very much like high school bullies. Maybe they were a new version of it. Something had brought out the worst in everyone.

Beverly said, "Coy ones are the most surprising, aren't they? They simply explode."

"I don't think it was the women who exploded last night," remarked Loretta.

"We heard you're setting up a sideline business, Carolina. I don't think you'll do well with your stable—I mean, personnel." This remark was from Frieda.

Everyone at the table looked shocked at the last two remarks—even Beverly. Carolina noticed that this was the first time Frieda had lashed out at all of them in such a direct and cruel way.

The Dining Room Manager came over to break up the crowd. *This behavior would not do here. Why they might even come to blows*, she thought.

"We need this table for the next seating. Please run along, ladies."

The three witches made their way out.

The other six looked at each other as if for confirmation of what had just happened and for comfort from each other.

Paula, the perfect lady who was required by etiquette to return Carolina's teatime hospitality, said, "I would like to invite you all to my place for tea at one tomorrow. Would you come? I'm serving just cucumber sandwiches and tea biscuits with lemon sauce. That's what I was out buying last night, anticipating your acceptance."

The others looked appreciative and surprised.

"Well, yes," "Thank you," "Of course," "Swell," "Can I bring anything?"

"I have everything, thank you."

"Let's get out of here," said Margie. "It's nice that cats like my Apolonia always like you."

They walked out in a line, Margie softly humming part of a song called, "Hold Your Head Up!"

On the way, they heard Mike loudly singing Da Da Da! to "The Stripper" while his coterie of poker buddies had a good laugh.

CHAPTER 17: AFTERNOON TEA AND EVENING FRENZY

The next day, Paula let Rita into her apartment, a nice two bedroom with model apartment furnishings.

"I see you still don't have your own furniture," noted Rita.

"Soon I will," replied Paula. "I don't want a lot of it here. Downsizing is hard."

Margie, Annie and Carolina arrived about the same time. Dot came last. They sat around Paula's dining room table, set just big enough for them. Paula had the table decorated with flowers, a beautiful tablecloth under the cloth napkins and dessert plates. She got the tea and coffee pots and a carafe of hot water, all Wedgwood. She brought out biscuits with lemon sauce and little cucumber and watercress sandwiches with the crusts cut off.

"Does anyone want decaf coffee or tea?"

"Yes," said a few, and were given decaffeinated loose tea in special pots with hot water.

"Thank you, Paula," someone said, and they all nodded.

The elegance took much concentration to keep things clean and unbroken. The food was delicious. Even Rita, who knew designer everything, was impressed by the way the tea was presented.

"Do you have everything you need for your apartment, Paula? We can loan you odd things you may need," said Carolina.

"No, thank you. I had to buy some things that a regular furnished apartment would normally have—like a broom and some special kitchen tools. Those things aren't in a model apartment."

"You have a pretty view here of those trees out there. They flower very beautifully," said Rita.

"Yes."

All of this conversation seemed boring to everyone but Paula.

"So are you happy here?" asked Dot.

"I could use more room. I have my computer in the bedroom, and lots of things from my old house that I'm going through to decide how to handle— keep, give away or throw away."

"I can show you the best way to get rid of things here. If you give it away, lots of people will just bring it back to you," said Rita who threw away very expensive items to prove she was not a hoarder.

"I can manage," said Paula succinctly, who would never be up for the title of "Toastmaster of the Year."

Carolina got up to use the bathroom and tried to get into the coat closet where she thought Paula had put her cane (more like an outdoor hiking stick) when she'd arrived, but the closet was locked.

"Your stick is behind the table in the foyer," said Paula, appearing suddenly. "I keep that door locked when the cleaner comes. I don't trust everyone. I lock my door to the main bedroom too in case anyone might want to go in there, where my jewelry is. I'll do that until I get my safe when my furniture is delivered."

"Thank you, Paula," replied Carolina, recovering from the slight shock. "I did want to use the bathroom. May I use the one across from your spare room?" Paula approved, so Carolina washed her hands in the small room and then got her stick.

Since talk had completely dried up, Carolina took her cup to the sink. Others helped clear the table carefully, got their things and left.

"That was OK," said Annie, once they were all in the hallway. "The food was good."

"Not much fun," said Dot decidedly.

Carolina was very pleased with the outing to Paula's, except for Paula's remark about the locked bedroom door that she might have misunderstood. "Paula went to a lot of trouble to make that food for us."

"Lucky for her she went shopping and missed movie night," said Margie, who'd not felt very welcome.

Later in the day, the group assembled for dinner. Annie came in last; people were starting to talk to her again since she was treating them in the friendly way she had before the Mike incident. Carolina saw this progress with equanimity. She believed the world eventually reverted to good if you just gave it time, although evil must still be battled whenever it appeared.

Annie came to the back table very excited, saying joyfully that she'd heard that Floyd was coming back—maybe even tomorrow.

"He keeps two apartments—one here and one in Florida," she told Paula. "There will be music in the entertainment room again!"

"I will enjoy meeting him if you like him so much," said Paula politely.

Margie smiled, remembering the tunes Floyd always played. "I hope he wears those snakeskin shoes."

"He will," said Dot. "He must have twenty pairs!"

They all left the dining room, turning toward the mail room to get their mail, Annie hoping for more company before the next movie. Suddenly, there was the tinkling sound of ivories.

"He's here!" "He's back!" cried voices from around the lobby. "Come on!" urged Annie.

Margie followed Annie, because she liked the old Tin Pan Alley music. Rita and Dot got their mail and left. Carolina followed Margie and Annie to hear Floyd—reluctantly. She was, for some reason, affected unwillingly by Ike's masculinity, but not by a slick playboy like Floyd.

The three women entered the room and sat down behind the piano to hear the same repertoire as last year. Carolina hoped that Floyd had learned more songs while he was down in Florida, but assumed that horses and women (in that order) had probably filled up his time to the hilt.

Floyd played and more people than usual sang along. Ike was there saying, "Play 'Once in a While,' Floyd." This time, Ike looked hopefully at his new girlfriend, Joyce.

Floyd loved being the belle of the ball. He was wearing a pink shirt, open at the top and a new pair of snakeskin shoes.

Eventually, people left to go to the second-seating dinner. Some called to Floyd to join them.

But Floyd played until it was too late to get his dinner.

Then, he got up, and Annie, Carolina and Margie stood up to say hello.

Floyd smiled in his devil-may-care way. He indicated that he'd play Annie's favorite song next time, which wasn't her favorite, but she didn't want to correct him.

He leered at the women before he left, looking at Carolina mostly.

"I hear you ladies like lap dances. I can do a good one for you anytime you want," he said, grinding his hips.

Annie laughed, waiting to see what else he would say. Carolina and Margie looked aghast.

Floyd hurried off, the fastest 93-year-old man that anybody had ever seen.

"Really, Annie," said Carolina.

"He's a musician, he may be a good dancer," said Annie, unrepentant.

Annie and Carolina went off to the central elevator to go to their rooms. It was not Carolina's nearest elevator but she enjoyed taking it up to Annie's floor, sometimes getting out to talk to her longer.

Margie stopped to check the movie poster in the lobby and to give the other two a chance to talk alone, knowing they enjoyed it. She wandered into the game room to see which games were still being played. There was a Scrabble game in progress. *Cursor—that was good word*, thought Margie. *Zip line?* She wondered who was athletic enough here to get that one, although in their boredom, the residents often watched anything on TV, and sometimes their grandchildren were doing interesting things like zip lining.

Suddenly, a woman approached her, saying something and it wasn't good. It was Frieda.

"Why are you here, Mrs. Belbuck? Everyone knows you were in prison and your husband left you. You don't even have hair! You should leave. You're probably not even paying your rent or you'd have better clothes!"

Margie stood terrified. Why was this woman terrorizing her?

"I wish I were in jail than here with you, Frieda!" she cried. It was all she could think of to say. "And my husband left me to chase other women. He was a player."

"If you can't keep your husband, it's your own fault!" screamed Frieda. "Men are fair game."

Margie, a conventional woman as far as marriage was concerned, looked with horror at

Frieda who'd suddenly turned crazy, it seemed. Was she hallucinating or had Frieda turned into some sort of fiend out for retribution? It didn't make sense.

During Frieda's tirade, Margie had worked her way around, until her back was to the door, then suddenly turned and ran as fast as she could, which was not very fast. She rushed to the Courte's front door, out to the sidewalk and then back to the entrance near the farthest elevator. She made it to her floor and ran towards her apartment. She got in and locked the door. Apie had hidden under the sofa, not used to his mistress's strange behavior.

Margie flung herself down on her bed and cried inconsolably, thinking she would never get used to such bizarre and unkind behavior. It was cruel to mention her ex-husband, really cruel.

But Margie's anguish was not over yet. A drastically unfortunate incident soon occurred that affected the well-being of all of the group and put finding desirable dining companions into perspective. Something happened to Margie— who seemed to be the lightning rod for attracting violence and social condemnation. This time, it was not even certain that she would ever get out of her morass. It puzzled even her friends.

CHAPTER 18: MAY I BORROW YOUR FACE?

The far wing of the first floor woke in the middle of the night to shouts of "Help!" and to the sounds of clattering as two women made their way towards the concierge desk. Mr. Howard was on duty again.

"Help! Call the police. I was accosted in the game room tonight by that Margie Belbuck, and later she was outside my window with her voodoo mask, putting a curse or worse on me! She's crazy. She should not be allowed to live here! She should be in jail where she came from!"

"Shhh! Frieda," said Paula who was with her. "Please have someone look around for a person outside of our windows. I too saw a mask at my window." She spoke quietly.

The concierge went out to take a look with a flashlight.

In the meantime, Carolina appeared at the desk in her terrycloth robe over her flannel nightgown. Loretta, nosey parker that she was, had called Carolina on her phone because she'd heard Frieda yelling something about Margie acting up again. Loretta thought that Carolina would want to hear about it, and she might make things even more interesting.

Paula came over to Carolina and drew her aside. "It's the masks. I don't know what to do after seeing that terrible face again. Frieda was scared and says she saw Margie out there. Carolina, I did too. She was outside my window, and I saw her under the light. I saw her clearly. What should I do?"

"Tell the truth, of course, Paula. But are you sure?"

"Yes."

The concierge came back, holding a thick cane with a glowing cardboard face on top.

"I found this. I think I must call Management, and they'll tell me to call the police. Did you actually see Mrs. Belbuck?" This question was directed to Frieda.

"Yes!" she shrieked. "I told you. I don't know why you're waiting. She should be put out of here!"

"Can you also identify the person who was outside your window?" This question was directed toward Paula.

"Tell him! You said you saw her too!" yelled Frieda, grabbing Paula's arm.

"Yes, I did. It was Mrs. Belbuck," Paula said sadly, with her head bent.

"I'll go upstairs and stay with her," said Carolina.

"And start some other plot! Oh, no, you don't!" screamed Frieda. "You're always getting her out of trouble, Carolina. If you want to help her, why don't you get her some better clothes and her hair fixed?"

Carolina left with the eyes of the small crowd that had collected focused on her back.

She went up to Margie's apartment and knocked on her door.

Margie peeked her head out a crack in the door. She was still in her day clothes, evidently not having changed after her run-in with Frieda in the game room.

"What is it?" She was being careful.

"Let me in."

Margie opened the door.

Carolina was horrified. Margie looked worse than when she'd been in jail. Her hair was matted on the side from her tears. Her clothes were beyond rumpled.

"What's wrong, Carolina?"

Carolina went in. "Let's sit down and have some tea. There was a little dust up tonight. Nobody was hurt. But we have to talk."

"Are the police coming to take me away?" Margie said this like it was inevitable.

"No, of course not. They might be here to ask you some questions. Let's talk and then you can wash up a bit and put on fresh clothes."

They sat at the dining room table.

"The mask made a comeback today at Frieda's and Paula's windows. Your name came up unfortunately by both women separately. Were you outside tonight, Margie?"

"No, no, Carolina. It wasn't me. I ran into Frieda tonight. She said terrible things to me and I fled up here and cried. Honest. I never left."

"I believe you. I'll stay with you. You should wash up now in case someone comes."

Margie got up like every bone and nerve of her body hurt. She moved slowly to her bathroom.

Apolonia came over to Carolina from her hiding place under the couch. "You're fine, little girl." Carolina soothed and petted her. "So is your adopted mother," she lied.

There was a knock on the door. Carolina answered it. It was a policeman.

"I'd like to speak to Mrs. Belbuck." He was one of the ones who'd been there already. He knew Margie by now.

"I'll get her."

But Margie had already come out.

"I didn't do it. I haven't left my apartment all night."

The policeman made notes and asked a few more questions. He said someone might be back. He looked at Carolina who said she hadn't been out of bed until someone called her on the phone to tell her the women who saw the mask were meeting in the lobby.

He left after having gotten the exact locations and times they both had been anywhere that night. He stayed in the hallway the whole time while he asked his questions.

"See, Margie," said Carolina. "No one was hurt. It was just some prank. We'll find out what it was all about, like last time. Something strange is happening here. Don't worry. You just take care of Apie. You are safe."

"Who would be using my face?" asked Margie. "Did they find a mask of my face that someone wore?"

Carolina did not say that anybody at the Courte had Margie's short plump body or could be mistaken for her. "I don't think so. It's just mistaken identity. Don't be afraid if people act like it was you. Some might be unkind or stay away from you. Do you want to go away for a while? I'll take care of Apie."

"No, I can't think. I just want to lie down. I'll think more about it tomorrow. I'll stay in here a few days."

"You might want to face them down," said Carolina.

"Maybe later. I just want to stay in here a while."

Carolina hugged her, waited for the chain to go up and went to her room. She thought maybe she could solve it all with some new information she was going to look into and not have to force Margie into a stare down contest. There was something she'd held back from Margie that broke Carolina's heart. Carolina got to her apartment and got ready for bed, not realizing she still had her net on that preserved her hard to maintain hair-do of old fashioned spit curls and precise waves.

CHAPTER 19: CAROLINA LEARNS SOME THINGS

In the morning, Carolina got dressed and decided to go to breakfast, but first she made a phone call to the police station and asked for Captain Dereck.

"Hello, Captain. There's something I have to tell the police that I couldn't last night since I was with another person, and you might want to keep it quiet."

"What is it, Carolina?"

"Just that the pole that the mask was attached to that scared the two residents last night was my cane. I don't think it was used the last time the mask appeared. I don't know how it got out there this time. I could have forgotten it someplace because I don't often use it and I just brought it out recently to carry sometimes."

"Your protection again, Carolina?" said Dereck. "You be careful. Is that all? A cane and nobody was hurt?"

"Yes, I know nothing more about what happened last night."

"I guess your friend with the cat could have gotten the cane at any time?" asked the Captain.

"So could the rest of the people at the Courte as far as I know, depending on where I left it. I can see this information doesn't help at all. I do want that cane back sometime, though. It's an heirloom," she said, sounding stern and hoping to deflect attention from Margie.

Carolina left her apartment and stopped at Margie's before she went to breakfast. Margie opened the door but was not dressed for the day.

"Do you have enough food, Margie?"

"I'm OK. I can stay here for a few weeks. I can order online. I have enough cat food too. Thanks, Carolina."

"You can certainly not stay in there for weeks. Your friends will not stand for it. We're humoring you right now." Carolina thought it was good for Margie to hole up and keep out of trouble, at least for a little while. She would get their friends to keep her company.

Carolina went to the lobby and looked around. She took a careful look at the concierge desk. She wondered if the residents' keys were locked up yet. But probably the key to the cabinet with the keys would be on the wall nearby.

She asked to speak with Angie, the aide to Management. The concierge said he would call.

"You can go back now," he said. Carolina opened the side door and went to the back. Angie met her by the copy machine so they wouldn't have to sit down probably, and Carolina would have to leave soon.

"What do you want, Ms. Pennsbury?"

"I was wondering if the carts are still back here in case I need one for a package I may be expecting. I don't know how heavy it will be."

"They're still here. Just ask the concierge to get you one when you need it. What do you really want, Ms. Pennsbury?"

"I wanted to see how things are set up now. I see the keys are in a cabinet. I was looking to see where the master key was. I didn't think everyone who works here would get one, but it has to be in an accessible place. I think it may be in the concierge desk."

"Maybe you're right," Angie said slyly.

"If I can get it, I imagine a lot of people can."

"Stop detecting, Carolina. You will stir up trouble again."

"Or save someone again."

"Or risk your own life again."

"Can someone come back here to get a cart whenever they want to like before?"

"They aren't supposed to, but you know how it gets when the concierge is busy. I didn't say that if anyone asks."

"Thanks, Angie. Anyone can get a key to any apartment. It means we're not safe in our own beds."

"Who do you think it is, Caro-, Ms. Pennsbury?"

Carolina knew Angie could risk her job by calling people by their first names, so she didn't mention Angie's slip. "If I find out, you'll be one of the first to know, as they say."

"Thanks."

Carolina left for breakfast and her forbidden detecting. She wondered what had happened to her walking stick that it could be used as part of the "mask-at-the-window" terror campaign. She wondered if anyone else had seen the mask incident from their windows.

"Hello, Joan. Hi, Joyce." (Joyce was sitting with Ike). Maxine and Milton went by. Loretta and Hazel were sitting with Beverly. Carolina looked around strategically. She made some tea at the beverage counter and toasted a bagel, putting them on a tray and then sat with some sewing circle people who were seated with Maxine and Milton.

"How's Margie?" they asked. "Why doesn't she come down?"

"She's tired. She'll come down soon." She sipped her tea. "I seem to have lost my cane. It's an old one, heavy, made of hardwood. Has anyone seen it? I don't use it often so sometimes I forget and leave it somewhere."

Gretchen said, "That's funny. I saw one like that in the corner of the library but thought it was there waiting for someone—or it could have been in the dining room. You know how we put things around the room near us when it's crowded. I remember a lot of people being around, so it was some kind of gathering. Did you ask at the concierge desk?"

"I looked there, but thanks."

"Are you having problems walking, Carolina?" Maxine asked.

"Some days a little support doesn't hurt."

"Mike might be leaving," said Milton. "He said there are too many fussy old hens, but he only says that when he's with the boys. He's one good poker player. I'd rather build models and I do sometimes when they're playing. They say the glue fumes bother them. They're fussy old hens themselves."

His wife Maxine said, "Milton is very creative. He did a model kit of the Three Musketeers. He says there's a fourth Musketeer—Dart something."

Milton preened and started telling one of his jokes. "What did the woodpecker do when..."

He was interrupted by Beverly who was going by, stopping to talk to Gretchen.

"Why don't you come and sew with us, Bev? Do you tat or knit or crochet?"

"You asked me that before," replied Bev. "That's for old women. Haven't you noticed? I'm young!" Beverly turned around precariously on her high heels. "I spend my time buying shoes in New York. I won't wear those old lady sweaters they make here anyway. They'd ruin my figure."

Gretchen looked angry. "I make those sweaters. We don't make ugly sweaters. We're better than professionals, and everything we do is handmade. Paula says they're a good investment."

Beverly moved on as Gretchen said to Carolina, "You haven't shown us your Aunt Ida's sampler yet. You did say you'd come back and show us. You were never known to lie, Carolina."

Judy, who was universally liked for her good nature and rapport with people, quickly added, "Of course, Carolina would never lie. I'm sure she's just busy and will get back to us to show us something special from her aunt soon."

"Yes, I'll be back soon. I have several things I'm getting together to show you."

The ladies looked pleased.

Carla, wanting some attention, said, "I live on the first floor and I'm never bothered by anyone like other people are," referring to recent happenings with the masks.

"Do you take your hearing aids out at night?" asked Carolina.

"Well, yes, but I can see."

"I think they tap the mask on the windows to get the person's attention to look out," said Carolina.

"You do have those thick thermal curtains too," Gretchen, her friend, said loudly.

"Well, yes, but so what? Everyone has curtains or shades and they wake up. I still say they're seeing things that aren't there."

"But the concierge found the mask outside," said Maxine.

"That could have been left anytime or dropped out of a window," suggested Carla. "Maybe someone was cutting the grass and had a mask in his pocket."

The others smiled.

"Don't laugh. Carla is usually right," said Gretchen to an incredulous audience. She added, "I'm making this sweater for Paula. She knows nice clothes when she sees them. She's paying me, although I don't need it. I wanted to make this sweater into a cat. Wouldn't that that be nice? With a crocheted cat collar where her necklace would be? But Paula said she hates cats."

Carolina looked surprised. Paula had seemed concerned about Margie's cat, although she did have expensive clothes and wouldn't want to get anything on them. Carolina couldn't see her wearing one of Gretchen's creations though.

Carolina left, having learned some things.

She went to her room, hearing her phone ring as she unlocked her door. She saw the strip she'd placed in her door still in the same place. She answered the phone to hear the Captain's voice.

"The police may be investigating Margie for the poisoning and for the harassment with the mask."

"I hope you'll be doing a general investigation. Margie is innocent of everything."

"Well, we don't want to arrest her yet since she was in jail by mistake the last time. The press might get involved. But her fingerprints were on the handle of the cane."

"Of course, they were. We hand each other our walking appliances all the time. Were mine on it? You have our prints from that last run in we had with the police—or the police had with us, to be more accurate."

"Yes, but only those two sets—yours and Mrs. Belbuck's—were clear."

"Isn't that strange? I'm sure a lot of people have touched that cane."

"Could your house cleaner have wiped it down?"

"Why? That's not her job. It sounds like someone tried to wipe it clean knowing where we had handled it. I think I lost it in the library or dining room and Margie must have leaned it against a wall or something using the handle. The person wanting to use it for the mask holder, picked it up somehow and wiped it down to get his or her fingerprints off it, not touching the handle. It did have other blurred prints on it too, I thought you said."

"The Police could only say that it was cleaned before, and that only you and Mrs. Belbuck touched it later. Maybe Mrs. Belbuck wiped it down, but her fingerprints got on it by accident while she was making the mask and then losing it outside, probably panicking because someone might have come out and found her that night. She was seen in the light. I shouldn't have told you about this, Carolina. I know Mrs. Belbuck is fragile and I wanted to warn you so you can keep an eye on her if something happens with the police."

"I have some ideas. Can you wait another day or two?"

"Well, since no one was hurt with this last incident, it doesn't have the highest priority. But I'll have to do what is required of me. I'm not the direct person in charge of this investigation."

Carolina got off the phone, almost in a panic herself. "Stop it! Calm down! You can't help anyone like this." Carolina sat down in her father's heavy revolving desk chair and faced the trees outside. She put her head on the desk, then raised it with determination. It was all a matter of faith and getting strength from those who'd loved her in the past and had not failed her, no matter how hard things were. She must have strength for others now.

She talked to herself out loud again. "Do I know enough to solve this? I must go by my instincts on this one since I have one main suspicion I can't get beyond. I must work backward this time from the most likely perpetrator to evidence exonerating Margie instead of from one logical step toward another. Let me think."

What was seen outside was odd but it was confirmed by two people independently.

Where were the frightening masks kept? Carolina did not subscribe to the idea that they were demons conjured up by voodoo.

Was Margie sleepwalking? Did she have a mental breakdown? Frieda was harassing Margie, but Frieda had started to harass everyone at the table. Why would Margie target Paula for a mask attack when Paula had come so recently to the table—after Mike and Frieda? And Paula seemed to be accepting of Margie. Was it to disguise who was the real target? Maybe the perpetrator (Carolina couldn't bring herself to say Margie) had probably hit more windows with the cane but residents probably hadn't seen or heard it. If the perpetrator did plan all of that, then it sounded like premeditation. So did making the signs. Would Margie take Carolina's walking stick? Carolina was her dear friend. She must have known it was Carolina's, but then again, other people had similar ones—the men anyway.

No, no, no! This doesn't make sense. Maybe work on the poisonings, and this other situation will work out. Maybe the mask business and the poisonings aren't connected, and Margie could get help for her derangement of some sort with the masks.

You aren't working the way you said you would. You have to adapt to circumstances, Carolina told herself. *You think you know who did it, and it wasn't Margie. Now figure out how and why.*

CHAPTER 20: MARTIAL LAW IS IMPOSED

Before Carolina could figure out the how and why of the Courte's affairs, she was delayed by the Courte's own attempt to figure out its own affairs. News of masks at windows and attempted poisonings and police involvement had gotten the attention of top management. But the clincher was the Courte becoming a laughing stock of all the retirement homes in the country by having sponsored a strip show—or so the rumor went. "Why would old folks want to see naked people anyway?" they asked. Some sort of perversion was spreading like a fungus in the place. They had recently hired an "enforcer" of rules to their team to keep the current lax management in line. The position was a new idea.

That was why residents sitting in the chairs in the lobby looked up one day as the light from the outside was darkened by a figure dressed in a dark fabric standing in the doorway of the entrance.

"Stalin is here!" Carla was heard to yelp in alarm.

"No, no. It's just some man in a dark suit," she was assured.

The man entered, looking straight ahead, but taking in everything and everybody. He walked to the concierge desk and turned on his heel toward the residents.

He said in a voice that made them shake, "I am sent from top Management because we care about you. I will get everything in shape according to rules. You will be happy. The bad will be re-educated."

He stepped forward one step but with aggression. Even Ike, sitting in the front row of chairs who'd been a gunner during WWII was afraid and covered his head. But the man wearing the suit that looked like a uniform, was not finished. He looked sternly at them, smiled with his lips only, and said, "Call me Ivan." He turned on his heel again and disappeared into the back offices. The concierge on duty dropped to his "at ease" military position.

Ivan scared both residents and staff for the duration of his stay. He never opened a door for himself, waiting for someone around him to open it. He walked with his arms at his side as if leading an army. Even people in wheel chairs rushed to open a door when Ivan was standing in front of one. The staff was quicker. Soon the staff were subdued, on time, polite to everyone, and every muscle in their bodies was tense.

One day, Margie went behind the concierge desk to get a cart for taking her cat litter package that she'd had delivered, to her apartment. She was stopped in her tracks to see all the carts padlocked. A note saying, "See Concierge for Cart" was attached to the lock.

Out of nowhere, Constantine, the new concierge, appeared in distress.

"Mrs. Belbuck, you must not be here. The carts are off limits. Please hurry back to the front."

Margie almost ran out in alarm.

"Do we have to pay or something?"

"No, but I'll pay if Mr. Ivan sees you. Please, please, forget I said that." Constantine looked around to see if anyone had heard.

Ivan, meanwhile, walked around the place, studying everything from ceiling to basement. Surveys on staff behavior were sent out to all residents, and Ivan showed up at the doors of those who did not send them back. He would enter as the door was opened for him, and look in every room to show that he was aware of residents' every move, although he always said he was looking for ways to improve the facility. He would wait as those poorest in health got up from their couches, found their walkers and opened the doors for him to leave, thanking him for searching their apartments, "Mr. uh, Ivan."

"Call me Ivan," Mr. "uh, Ivan" said. Residents who had other places to go, visited their families; some made plans to go to Florida—in the summer even. Cruise lines were bombarded with last minute requests to go anywhere—even to the Antarctic. Only travel to the Soviet Union was avoided.

Some of the disgruntled pointed to Margie behind her back and said, "She's the one who was reading *The Communist Manifesto*. Maybe she had something to do with him coming here." Carolina had been right about telling Margie to read that book in private.

Days went by, until Mr. "uh, Ivan," called a meeting for residents and staff in the dining room. Staff had to stand at attention around the room. The residents sat in chairs in rows—the residents that were still there, that is.

Ivan came in the door with notes in his hands. Some of the staff saluted, although Mr. Ivan was displeased with this behavior and wrote it down. The called him Mr. Ivan. Apparently, his name was Ivan Ivan, as far as any of them could figure out.

He stood up facing the entire group. He spoke with a slight eastern European accent.

"I am displeased at some things I have seen here. I expect them to change as I announce them. First, we will have an apology."

Poor Mr. Howard left the side of the room to stand by Mr. Ivan.

"I ask your forgiveness for using items not mine when I worked behind the concierge desk. I am a most unappreciative man and not worthy of your forgiveness." After an acceptable look from Mr. Ivan, Mr. Howard started to return to his place when he suddenly stopped and said very quickly, "I was going to replace the items as soon as I was off duty!" and returned to his place as Mr. Ivan made a move towards him but changed his mind.

"More confessions, I mean, apologies, will be forthcoming in days to come. I order you all to write down violations you make and inform me of those others make. There is a locked box with a slot specifically for this purpose in the mail room. Do not attempt to breach its security since surveillance is now installed everywhere at the Courte. You are safe now."

"Mr. Constantine is no longer with our little country—I mean, community. He must stand as a lesson of speaking out of turn. We have ways of finding out."

"I have names here of eleven residents who have taken carts out of the back room without asking the concierge. There is no time for public apologies today, but you will all write a letter and post it on the bulletin board which will be expanded." Ivan read the eleven names.

"Here is a list of fines for residents seen sleeping in the library and for asking for personal assistance from maintenance personnel. Mrs. Mealey, you are accused of trying to bribe our chief engineer to install an illegal device in your apartment, a most serious offense. You will be required to wear a sign saying so for one day."

People gasped.

Ivan continued, "You all have now seen that there have been no poisonings, no excess spending on days of celebration, and no striptease shows under my leadership. You will all write letters of thanks to me which I will forward to the Chairman...of the Board of the company. In the future, May Day will be acknowledged with a parade instead of any Cinco de Mayo parties with mariachi bands."

"You will all now please stand out of respect for our community and its leaders."

Annie stood up, but said, "No, we won't." She back down. "This is America. I fought for this country in WWII and I won't listen to you!"

Carolina stood up with her friend. "We must have been asleep. You're just a throwback, Ivan."

Dot stood up with her friends. "Maybe they used hypnotism to get us to go along."

Margie said, "Maybe it was cult programming. How do you like being denounced, Mr. Ivan?"

Rita, who had money, pointed at Ivan saying, "Forget denouncing. My lawyer will sue you and your company."

Soon, Mr. Ivan Ivan with his distinctive mustache and piercing eyes backed down as the bully he was. He backed out of the dining room and the hallway, then turned and ran for his office.

But already, a formal letter was on his desk saying he was fired and would be responsible for any losses his behavior had caused. A list of withdrawals of almost half of the Courte residents followed along with a list of people suing.

The Board members all blamed each other for Ivan's hiring, although three out of five of them had been on vacation at the time. Three out of five of them were always on vacation.

Notices of regret were sent to all residents who soon came home, cancelling all of their trips.

Cameras were removed from hallways and secret places. The days, or rather the two weeks, of someone's old version of totalitarianism were over. (Police spent hours studying the video feed locked in Mr. Ivan's office, more to check up on the suspicious Mr. Ivan's activities than interest in the poisoning of a cat. However, they did check.)

Floyd came back from Florida saying, "I just couldn't stand that summer Florida weather." Really, he'd had his eye on a new sales representative he met before he left. Nothing could deter Floyd from his rounds.

Beverly, who'd just gotten out of a limousine she'd hired to bring her back from a trip to her daughter's house, inhaled the air of freedom blowing though the Courte, and noticed that Ivan was gone. "What happened to Lochinvar?" she asked.

CHAPTER 21: CAROLINA BREAKS AND ENTERS

Getting back to finding out how and why herself, Carolina left her apartment, dressed in a dark skirt and blouse, as if it mattered. She felt it was easier dressed this way to think of herself playing the cloak and dagger game, as the women had who'd come to her tea. Then she wouldn't feel so afraid. But this trip wasn't fun; it could be embarrassing at least, or downright dangerous at worst.

Her purpose was to prove that someone could get hold of the keys to anyone's apartment easily and get in the apartments with planning. She intended on entering the apartments of the three new people who had or were now occupying the sixth seat in the far corner of the Buckingham Courte for Seniors.

As she walked down the corridors, it was hard not to look guilty. Dinner was over several hours ago. It was quiet time at the Courte. People were in their apartments relaxing, and only a few wanderers had yet to come home. The movie was playing, but there were no intermissions once the DVD started. If she were seen in places forbidden to residents, excuses would not be easy to come by. But would doubt a resident with a good excuse for being behind the concierge desk? Carolina comforted herself by asking. But someone with a suspicious mind could always come by unexpectedly wherever she might go. Late night would be a better time to try this experiment of getting the keys, but then the residents she most wanted to investigate would be home.

Tonight, she thought, *she'd hit the jackpot.* Mike would be out drinking as usual, Frieda had told someone she was visiting a friend, and Paula was out for some late shopping. Trifecta.

Carolina didn't expect to find out much in the apartments she would try to enter. She was sure the guilty person was smart enough to hide his or her tracks since workers could enter the apartments for many reasons. Most of them probably had a locked drawer or cabinet that would be hard to jimmy without leaving traces. This expedition was more of a test to see if she could enter apartments with impunity. She thought maybe that was how her walking stick had been acquired from Carolina's own apartment. The thief didn't have to see how they had touched the stick to know that Carolina's and maybe Margie's fingerprints would be on the handle. The thief was safe as long as he or she didn't touch the handle or wipe the part clean that he or she had touched. Whatever was left was gravy.

Carolina got to the main floor and reconnoitered. She saw no one in the mail room or in the hall on the side of the concierge desk. She could see that the movie was on but the glass door was darkened so she couldn't see inside. The game room and card room were empty. She turned the corner to see the concierge reading behind the desk, but nobody was in the library across from the desk. It was a slow weeknight. She said hello to the concierge, this time a young man recently hired. He said, "Hello, Miss Pennsbury." The new people were taught to learn all of the names of the residents. They did a good job. If only he would be called away for a time. He usually was; the job was very demanding except late at night. She sat in the library to wait for her chance.

Carolina wondered if she should have tried for the keys at either a very busy time when there was activity everywhere or in the middle of the night when the concierge took a break. With the keys in hand and at the ready, she could enter an apartment anytime someone was out. It was unlikely anyone would notice one key gone. She remembered that many of the apartments had two of the same keys hanging on a slot. She thought she might have to reconsider her plan unless luck or Providence shown upon her and her somewhat devious plan. She comforted herself with a reminder that detecting sometimes required necessary subterfuge. She would try to keep within the limits of necessity. But with Carolina adventuring out on this plan, Margie might not be the only one being carted off jail.

A taxi had pulled up to the front of the building. A resident with a disability would perhaps need assistance from the concierge. One did! The taxi driver came in asking for assistance with Mrs.

Bloomfield. Good old Evie! She had sent a message with the taxi driver saying she needed a wheelchair. The concierge would get the folding one left in the back for this purpose. He wheeled it out. If only no one else came by, if only no one got off the elevator, if only no one came out of the entertainment room. There seemed to be countless possibilities for disclosure. *Why had she thought it would be so easy?*

It was now or never or maybe later when she had thought of a better plan. She decided to take her chance. She stood up, went to the front door next to the concierge desk and back offices, and opened it. She hurried down the small passage still in view of the lobby and then reached the copy machines in safety. She looked for a key to the new locked cabinet containing the residents' keys, but couldn't find one on the tables or in the drawers. Ah! In the concierge desk! But going there was dangerous. She thought she heard sounds in front. She looked for a place to hide. She slipped into the clothes closet for the day workers that also held the carts that residents used for carrying packages to their rooms. She didn't have the heart to close the closet door the whole way. Now she'd be in trouble if someone found her hiding here. It would have been wiser to pretend she was there for some good reason like searching for the concierge or for a cart. Looking aboveboard with confidence and a good excuse was the better way. But here she was hiding in a closet. She'd better close the door. Oh, crap! (This was about the roughest expletive Carolina ever used.) The inside of the door had rattled.

She sat on the empty umbrella stand and felt for what had rattled the door to find—*the* key hanging on the back of the closet door. *Wasn't that convenient?* she thought to herself.

She grabbed the key. It must be *the* one, although she couldn't see the label. *Please let it be the one.* She could tell it had been recently made by feeling the rough new grooves with her fingers. This must be a copy they'd just made.

She took it and now had the courage to peek out of the door. Nobody was in the office area. She got up, went over to the new cabinet, and silently tried the key. It turned! Now what? What if the door squeaked? She opened it slowly. She knew she had to hurry. The concierge would be returning, maybe bringing the wheelchair back. Maybe she'd be lucky and he'd take Mrs. Bloomfield to her room if she was weak today.

Carolina opened the door to the large wall cabinet. Each apartment had a number with one or more keys hanging under it. She looked for the three apartment numbers she had memorized. She got one, then two, but the third wasn't there. It was out for some reason. It was Paula's, so maybe it was out because Paula had a model apartment or something. All of the residents had been back here to get their keys at one time or another when they'd been locked out in the past in the old days when the cabinet had been unlocked. Maybe Paula just hadn't returned hers to the concierge as she was instructed. Anyway, that was the best that

Carolina could do. She'd have liked to see into Paula's locked rooms. Of course, Paula's reasons for them being locked were logical and believable. Carolina put the two keys in her large pocket, the clothes being chosen for the occasion, the style for breaking and entering and hiding things.

She locked the cabinet door and put the cabinet key back on its hook.

She listened for noises at the desk. She heard the concierge talking! There was no way out. Then Carolina remembered that the side door leading from the offices might only be locked from the outside. Those rules about fire safety. Her nerves were making her stupid. She tried the door as the noise of the concierge could be heard coming toward the passage that led to the back where she was. The knob turned in her hand. She slipped out. She hoped the door closed before the concierge could see it had moved. Then she looked both ways in the hall. No one was there to see. She moved quickly, hoping no one from the movie room had looked out where the side door was visible. She went on to the back elevator on that side. So far, so good, except for Paula's apartment.

Carolina decided she had to do what she needed to as quickly as possible. That meant searching Frieda's apartment first since her return time was probably the most questionable. Carolina walked over to the farthest elevator on the other side and took it up to another floor where she was less likely to be seen walking across the corridors. She then took the elevator on the other side to the first floor again. She walked towards the apartment with the appropriate key hidden in her hand. She looked both ways down the hallway, hoping Frieda hadn't somehow gotten back, and hoping the Courte didn't still have hidden cameras in the halls. Or maybe they should but not now. Just as she was about to open the door, Paula came out of her nearby apartment! "Heaven be praised," as one of Carolina's old aunts used to say, for not having been able to get Paula's key. Carolina could have been caught red-handed or whatever body part might have been forfeited for sneaking into Paula's apartment while she was there to catch her.

"Hello, Carolina."

"Hello, Paula."

"I just got back from shopping. I'm off to get my mail. Would you like some iced tea?"

"I was taking a walk for exercise. Yes, I would," she smiled.

Paula looked disappointed, but opened the door for Carolina. Paula's closet was opened a bit, and from the glimpse Carolina could see, it seemed to be stacked with household goods like Paula had said. Paula obviously had many beautiful things. It must be difficult to choose from them. Paula closed the closet door before going to the kitchen saying she hated messes. Carolina knew that to be true from her appearance and from the state of the rest of her apartment. They sat at the dining room table and drank tea poured from an elegant pitcher into elegant matching glasses served with cloth napkins. Carolina drank it hurriedly, asking Paula a few questions about the quality of her day. She probably would not have learned anything more had she gotten Paula's key. Paula had seemed comfortable about asking her in. The locked doors were probably as innocent as the explanations Paula gave for them. Carolina left, saying Paula probably had a lot to do.

They left together, but turned opposite ways. Carolina watched Paula go off and turn the corner before she turned the key, breaking and entering into Frieda's apartment. After she got in, she had to decide which lights to turn on. She decided to use lights, choosing speed for searching instead of stealth in the dark. She looked in drawers and cabinets and under bathroom sinks. Carolina found nothing suspicious, although a good hiding place could still be well-hidden and missed. Frieda's drugs looked like the normal ones for a person her age. Carolina saw a letter on a desk that looked like it was from a sister whose health was failing. There were letters from some part of Austria too. Nothing was hidden in cupboards or in dryers or under throw rugs. One bureau was locked, but that was normal in a place that was not your own. One wouldn't want to keep all valuables in the bank's safe deposit box. Carolina made sure the lights were as they were when she'd entered, then she opened the door a crack and stepped out. She locked the door as it had been and quickly walked down the corridor.

She went to Mike's side of the building, looked both ways and entered. She was getting good at this. She listened, standing inside the door so she could escape if she heard Mike. No sound. She found unpaid bills and empty whiskey bottles and lots of clutter but nothing incriminating as far as poisons or motives. The most poisonous thing she'd found had been the amount of alcohol in the place. She left with great relief at her deliverance.

Perhaps deliverance had not come soon enough. As she left, she saw Hazel walking down the hall towards her. Carolina bent over as if looking on the floor in front of Mike's apartment.

"What are you looking for, Carolina?"

"The top of my keychain fell off as I was taking a walk. I thought I saw something shiny as I was retracing my steps. I guess it isn't here. How are you, Hazel?"

"Fine. I'm going home to see my favorite TV show, 'The Bachelor.' I'm already late. Do you watch it?"

"Not this season," said Carolina, wishing Hazel hadn't asked her something about a show to find out her white lie.

Hazel walked on. Carolina hoped she'd deflected Hazel's attention, *not hard to do with Hazel*, she thought somewhat guiltily but thankfully. Or else Hazel had fooled her, and the news would spread by tomorrow that Carolina had been seen furtively coming out of Mike's apartment. A sex scandal! What could she do about it now? She knew the chances she was taking. Some people already thought she had engaged strippers anyway.

Instead of heading back to the concierge desk to return the keys, Carolina walked back to her apartment in a state of exhaustion, both emotionally and physically. She got there without incident and dropped into her favorite armchair.

She thought a long while. What had she discovered by her herculean efforts? First, that she preferred to use her mind and find clues through speech instead of the Dashiell Hammett kind of detecting. It was Miss Marple for her, not Sam Spade. Second, that she had probably found nothing out by the expeditions to the apartments except that Mike was pretty much as she'd thought and Frieda better. Paula seemed to be as vacuous as usual but friendly. Carolina had found no real evidence, although she had had real suspicions. Third, that a resident could wait for an appropriate time and get to the key box, although it was somewhat harder now than before the keys were locked in a cabinet. Almost anyone could do it though, especially if they picked the right time. Carolina had tried to do it all in one evening. Even if one got caught, an excuse could usually be made like being locked out of one's apartment and not wanting to bother the concierge. She might have to use that excuse when she tried to return the keys. She dozed for a few hours.

Carolina knew about the change of shifts at night. She woke to leave her apartment and take the steps down to the first floor. She approached the concierge desk quietly. About 15 minutes before the shift change, she saw the concierge leave to go to his locker in the employees' lounge located near the mechanical room on the first floor. She hoped the fresh concierge was not early. She slipped in the back room and opened the cabinet and returned all of the keys to their appropriate hooks. She looked down to see some packages ready to go out the next day via UPS. They looked like packages from Paula according to the return addresses. Paula seemed to have lots of relatives but few if any visitors. Of course, she was just in the process of moving in.

Carolina saw that the coast was clear and slipped out of the door, missing both concierges who greeted each other as she was panting in distress just out of sight. She made it home without seeing anybody. Her prayers that night were ones of gratitude for her escapes and of mercy for her possible wrongdoings.

She prayed also that no evil one was searching behind the concierge desk tonight for keys to her apartment and that all of her friends had chains up on their doors. Had she seen any pliers on her visits that night she wondered?

She woke in the morning, knowing a lot more than she had the night before. Perhaps God was sending her wisdom. Suddenly, she remembered something someone had said some time ago. She connected it to the present circumstances. She knew and she knew why. But how did they do it? Carolina knew she must solve this problem quickly and creditably, not only to save Margie from an investigation and possible incarceration but to save them all from more attempts on their lives, this time not only Margie and Carolina. They had all been in danger, this killer was ruthless and careless of who got caught in the middle. That was proved.

CHAPTER 22: THE LULL BEFORE BATTLE

Carolina made some calls. Margie heard, "You must come down to dinner, Margie, please. It's important to me and to you." She called more people to be sure they were coming to dinner that night and to tell them to go along with what she was saying and to be sure to speak reasonably loudly so people at other tables could hear them. Then she went down to eat, or rather to something forbidden—detecting. The words of Angie and the Captain echoed in her head, although she'd tried to explain to them why she had to do it. But was she just being a foolish know-it-all who was wrong, or was she a person poking with a stick at a killer? Maybe she should wait for the police to find out what was wrong—after five or more funerals, including her own.

She'd borrowed a cane from a friend saying she had misplaced hers and walked towards the elevator to the dining room with a voice calling after her saying, "Don't lose this one, Carolina!" Little did they all know how she took the meaning of that to heart.

She sat as usual and the conversation was as usual. Margie was there at her request. She was a mess, but she was present.

Margie was talking like she usually did when she was very upset, about old movies, and the universe on String Theory, and whatever else she thought of. Paula was getting her first real taste of rambling Margie in a crisis.

"I was watching a movie called *Ladies They Talk About* the other night and Nan—in the movie—sees someone rushing and says, 'always in a hurry, and in here for life' or something like that. I think she was played by a young Barbara Stanwyck. It applies to us, doesn't it? Did I tell you it took place in a prison? They were in prison."

Everyone frowned at Margie, finding the comparison disparaging.

"How is your book coming, Margie?" Carolina asked to change the subject. Margie was writing a book about her past experiences with her husband and his many women. A quick thought passed Carolina's way that she wished it were a happy book about Margie's current experiences and her late husband, but she felt a pang of guilt.

"Not well. I'm not a good writer, I think. That's surprising, don't you think? I should be an artist; I have the temperament for it."

"Oh, you mean gloomy," said Annie. "I'd say you're more like a character *in* a book I used to read to my children—Eeyore."

Margie ignored this remark with no bad feeling taken.

"Maybe your book is good; you haven't let anyone read it critically yet," said Carolina.

"I saw a show about two kinds of multiple universes and what came before the Big Bang. Something about inflationary and gravitational waves. The scientists are sending up some probe that may test to see if there are such waves. I found the cyclic theory more interesting. Our universe will expand (by the influence of dark energy) until it's a thin membrane like others around it. The membranes bang into each other and more planets will fall out. Universes are created perpetually and then form more membranes. There was something about time keeping the membranes apart. Time does something. They say astrophysicists forget the concept of time when they think of these universes colliding. There's a cycle. I get things mixed up so I hope the show is repeated. I was fascinated by the idea of new universes being formed on the ends of enormous black holes—it seemed they were like big black spiders to me. Kind of creepy. Did anyone see the show so they can explain it better?"

Everyone was busy rolling their eyes at each other.

They ate their food, hoping Margie would shut up. Carolina knew that Margie was just nervous and was watching too much TV.

Suddenly, Carolina said, "I think we should all go away for a bit. I have friends who have invited us to stay with them. Even Apolonia. We need to get out of here. I hear some people are leaving for good. I hate to do that too soon. What do you think? Their house is wonderful. We can go the day after tomorrow."

"I don't know, Carolina. I was thinking of leaving for good," said Margie. "I feel afraid."

"We don't have to be afraid if we're away from here. We could walk in the woods or just enjoy the view from their deck."

"I was thinking of staying with my daughter if things got worse," said Annie. "I'm leaving for a few days."

"Was I invited to the country house too, Carolina?" asked Paula.

"Of course, or I wouldn't have asked at the table. You're one of our dining companions now."

"Well, I can't go at this time, thank you."

"I guess the trip won't work for all of us. I might go, anyone else?"

No one answered.

"I lost the bad prose contest," said Margie. My son said I must be a really bad writer to lose that. Not even a 'dishonorable mention.' My other friend said, 'What are you complaining about, Margie? That proves you can't write bad prove even if you try.' I don't know. It makes me feel depressed. I wanted to be mentioned. I tried really hard."

Margie rambled on. "I'd like to go to a feminist retirement home. Why don't feminists have old age homes? Why don't feminists help each other so women who've been hurt because they trusted men can be reminded they took the wrong path? I mean, they could have at least one home for women with husbands who leave them when they're old and sick."

"Probably feminists loyal to the cause don't have husbands like that. I don't think they'll get too many people like those you're talking about. Aren't we good enough for you? Some of us are feminists in a way," said Dot.

"Don't include everyone," said Annie. "Some of us were happy being wives and mothers."

Rita nodded.

"Oh, you mean happy to be oppressed," said Dot, who was teasing.

"Stop arguing, children. We're all proud women, happy to know each other at this time of our lives," said school teacher Carolina, who didn't need arguing at present.

"I'm reading several books now about women who were left like I was. It may become the new issue," Margie continued.

Annie ignored her. "I was adjusting my TV last night to get rid of some captioning that suddenly appeared. Now everyone is orange. If I try to change it by pushing other buttons, I lose cable altogether. Does anyone know what to do about orange people?"

""I'll help you, Annie," said Carolina. "If we can't manage it, we can call someone later."

"But I'll be leaving soon for my trip."

"I forgot."

Margie set off on a tangent again. "I was in bed the other night and saw my basket of laundry in the bathroom light. It's a round basket, wider at the top. A big white sheet was on top of the laundry and the whole thing looked like a wonderful chocolate cupcake with white icing so nicely spread, very thick and creamy."

"You think about food a lot, don't you?" asked Paula.

"I thought everyone does."

They all agreed to meet the next night for dinner since they might disperse for a time after that, who knew at their ages, maybe forever.

Carolina picked up a heavy walking stick and left with the others. She went to Margie's apartment to be sure she put her chain up and ate or drank only safe substances, bottled beverages or tap water, she warned. "And Apie too," she added.

Carolina walked back to her apartment, being very aware of her surroundings. She had the feeling of time repeating itself and started to think of Margie's explanations of those shows about string theory and parallel universes. She felt the same fear as when she'd walked the halls in the dark during the blackout. "Buck up, Carolina, your imagination is getting out of control." She said it the way one talks to oneself out of fear at a nightmare or to convince oneself that the pain one feels at 2 A.M. is not fatal. Suddenly, on her own floor she thought she saw Mike come out of the exit at the end of the hall she was walking down, walking heavily towards her. There was no escape. It was his shape, but he looked more beastly than his normal self. She walked with her head up, ready to meet her Maker. She was ready with her borrowed stick also.

But it was Dr. Mayer from another floor, who was probably visiting someone down the hall and taking the steps for his health. Instead of fighting for her life, she exchanged pleasant greetings with a harmless neighbor.

She was glad to get to her apartment, wishing again it was not so isolated. A person could scream her head off and not be heard. Someone could sneak up a nearby exit using a key to her door filched from behind the concierge desk—locked cabinet or not. The concierge just had to go to the restroom and you were a goner. She'd suggest getting a panel with a code but they'd post the code in the same area. She entered her apartment and looked in the mirror near the front door. *How tired and old she looked*, she thought. She checked out her apartment for intruders, even the closets. She put her own chain up.

She sat in the half-light thinking of how things could go wrong.

Were we being harassed in the legal sense by Mike? Was he menacing them? But the schemes taking place seemed dangerously sneaky, not ones using force or pranks.

Carolina got up to look out of the window. Life could be so beautiful. Why were they risking themselves to stay here? She guessed it was to stay together. They had families but needed lives of their own. Family and friends visited when they could. The group needed each other for the lives they lived when no one was visiting. Carolina remembered the first time Annie had written Carolina's name on a communal get-well card when Carolina was not available to sign it. Carolina had felt like family when someone thanked her for the card. It had touched Carolina. Annie's confidence in signing her name touched her heart and she trusted Annie not to go too far. It had made this effort to keep each other safe and together worthwhile.

Carolina made a few more calls that night and prepared for battle tomorrow. She wished she could wear Dot's battle helmet hat. She thought about Shakespeare's plays for a long time and one play in particular. She needed something to help her not feel her age. She remembered a time when she'd been in her prime like Jean Brodie and nothing in her body hurt.

CHAPTER 23: THE TRUTH OUTS

Carolina made some preparations in the morning. She ate breakfast in her apartment. She sat at her desk just to meditate and see what thoughts came, maybe good wishes, maybe a warning.

She found herself thinking again of how much she liked eccentric people as long as there was an innocence about them. Innocence had nothing to do with lack of sex or youth or prettiness. Her friends all shared some kind of innocence, a willingness to trust and accept new people and their ways.

She looked up that quote she had forgotten awhile back. It was from *Henry IV, Pt. 2.* "The wish was father, Henry, to that thought" said by the King. The son was taking the crown from his "dead" father's head when the "dead" father spoke up. Carolina had looked it up on the computer, although she had the complete plays, as complete as we could have them. In the old days, she would have used a bulky concordance to look up key words in important books. But computers were the thing these days. They were quick and efficient, but was the information they generated always so accurate? Of course not. One had to interpret sources and there were lots of people out there abusing the computer, bullying, lying, misinterpreting. Just look at what had happened to Margie's marriage. We were throwing innocents into this minefield of the internet. *Not that Margie's womanizing husband had been an innocent,* Carolina conceded. But Margie was, and was secondarily abused by the people who set up those databases to make sex partners easily available to people like her husband who was so lazy he used the easy way to find females. And he waited until he safely had lots of them before he dumped his wife. What a coward he was.

Almost all of the people here had access to a computer. There was one in the library that was slow. Most of those who used computers had their own internet access. They shopped, looked things up, communicated with friends and used them as word processors. Annie didn't. What about Mike, Frieda, Paula, Ike, Loretta and the others?

She then worked around her apartment doing chores, called church friends, and also called to invite her police friend to be a dinner guest that night but to sit at another table.

Could anything go wrong? She thought awhile again and knew how many things could.

She took a nap. She got up and got ready.

Tonight was Chef's Night. Everyone would go to the carving table and choose from a special buffet. Most went up again later to choose a dessert. People were moving around all of the time. Even the people with walkers got up to look at what was offered although they might ask a server or friend to bring it. Many put their selections on the shelf they had in their walkers. The servers had more time to serve individuals since most people served themselves. So drinks flowed and there was much moving around by servers and residents. It seemed to be chaos until all of the diners were seated in their chairs and eating. She had cautioned her friends accordingly. Carolina had picked this night of commotion to test suspicious people and was lucky that one such free-for-all day had just come up. Maybe it was a sign or a blessing that she was doing the right thing.

All six were there in their seats, having survived the lines and chaos. The usual people sat around them at their own tables. Most people came for Chef's Night. The server came over with water, and Carolina proposed a toast after asking for fresh glasses. The server surprisingly didn't say a word but brought them.

"Here's to friendship and protection from those who would harm us or our souls."

They drank fresh water from fresh glasses.

"That was kind of preachy," said Dot.

"It depends on what I was praying for. I could have meant it was for our own well-being and sense of self-preservation as a family."

"You didn't say so."

"One must interpret what one hears or reads even more these days with computers and television spouting every kind of message. You know something about that, Margie."

"Dream girls more or less popped right up on the internet for my ex."

"Maybe not dream girls, Margie. You didn't talk to them a lot."

"Do you use the computer frequently, Paula?"

"Sometimes." She drank her water with lemon quickly.

"I see you get lots of boxes."

"You know I'm sifting through my belongings to choose what I need now."

"I don't think so. I looked at the boxes you send and saw that some were being mailed out to different people. They look like professional mailings."

"So, I'm giving my things away to my relatives. Why are you asking these questions?"

"Because you are the poisoner."

"That is inaccurate and impolite. I'm surprised at your lapse of manners, Carolina."

"You came here for revenge against Margie. You have an online selling business that uses a service that asks for customers for ratings. Margie gave you a bad rating, for a good reason. She talked to us at dinner once about getting nasty responses in the mail and online. You have been planning to hurt Margie for a long time. You knew her home address since you'd sent the original package she had purchased. You now have a lower rating and don't have the prestige that you so wanted. I've read some of those warnings and pleadings from sellers to give only good ratings. Some sounded like fanatics. I think you are one."

"Why would I go to all of that trouble for *her*?" Paula asked with derision.

"Because you are looney tunes."

Paula's body started to blow up in appearance. Her groomed little self started to look like a female version of the Incredible Hulk. She was breathing through her nose like a bull. She reached for a glass of water on the table.

Carolina said, "Are you sure that's the safe one?"

Carolina turned to the others and said loudly, "She could have poisoned one or more of the drinks. That's why the rest of us are sticking to the ones just poured by the server."

People around them, especially the Captain at a table nearby in a little alcove, listened carefully.

"I suspected it was you when you invited us over for tea. You had your bedroom and coat closet doors locked. You made good excuses about being afraid of theft and sifting through your possessions that I believed for a little while after I saw into your closet the night we had iced tea. But then I thought, what if it's a computer business you were hiding? No one I've ever known moves their things in the way you claimed, especially such a meticulous person. Then you hired Gretchen to make sweaters for you, thinking you could make a profit selling them as handmade items."

"You learned our ways. You knew Margie got regular grocery deliveries. Following the delivery man, you put the doctored tuna packet in one of Margie's bags while the man was someplace else with the other bags. You did not know that the cat food would not be delivered. You wanted the tuna for Margie or whomever else she served it to in her apartment. It didn't work. Apie ate some and had to go to the animal hospital."

"Then you knew the days the pharmacy delivers. Sometimes a concierge will accept a delivery if the person is not available and will have the person sign for it later. You tampered with Margie's stomach medicine using the eye drops. I presume you were starting to give other poison such as anti-freeze to Margie too, in different ways. The concierge had the stomach flu and was away from the desk a lot that night, so you could do whatever you wanted to the medications. He took a high dose of the stomach medicine and collapsed. People somehow blamed Margie irrationally. But Mr. Howard survived."

"You needed to cover your tracks and get rid of the eye drops and packaging that came with the stomach medicine. So you got masks you had in your inventory and climbed out of your window and scared Frieda with them and then ran back to your apartment. Both of you are on the first floor. I'd wondered why the mask attacks didn't spread. They were just a ruse to give you an alibi of sorts and were part of your plan to have Margie suspected. You also had an excuse to get up that night and come out to the desk. You got the packaging and tried to dispose of it, being careful to get rid of fingerprints you might have left, then you called Management for help. There was a lot of confusion that night."

"You took my cane from my room for the next time you used the masks, throwing suspicion on Margie and using your mask trick the night that Frieda cornered Margie in the game room. You screamed in your room that night and ran to Frieda's apartment asking her if she'd seen Margie using the masks. She said yes. You had put that image into her mind and she wanted to believe it; she did believe it. You may have been putting some sort of drug in something you gave Frieda to drink since she's been getting more aggressive. A steroid?"

"If the police check our glasses now, I'm sure they'll find one or all of our first drinks were tampered with. We were careful to get all of our food from the buffet and watch it too."

(Still the other women at the table looked askance at their food.)

"And if they check your apartment, I'm sure they'll see your professional business, which, by the way, is forbidden here. I remembered that conversation Margie had with us about the trouble she was having with a seller. I suddenly knew the motive. The police can check your computer for any transactions or notes you sent Margie in the past about the sale. I'll bet you have all sorts of poisons in your locked bedroom in addition to the anti-freeze you used in the tuna."

Paula got up. Luckily for her, the tweed suit she wore quickly expanded to fill her new form, the bloating hatred spreading through her, her face bulging and red.

"I hate you, Carolina, and I hate you, Margie! You didn't write to me before you gave that review! I wanted 100%. I've spent a fortune to get even with you! I hate cats and I hate listening to you about your ex. And, Carolina, you are a, a *busybody*! I wish I'd bashed you with that cane when I had it. It would have been *so* appropriate. And why won't you eat poison? I put enough around your apartment!"

By now, it was obvious to everyone that she was crazy as a loony bird.

The Captain was behind her, taking her by the arm to the front area. He'd already called other officers to come. Paula was led through the lobby to a police vehicle and taken out of their lives.

The Police marked the dining room as a crime scene and escorted residents out, not letting them touch any food.

"What about the second seating?" the chef asked.

It was agreed to serve them sandwiches from the kitchen in the library and other rooms up front.

Everyone was mad at Carolina for this until it was suggested she might have saved them from a mad poisoner. But it was a close call. The residents loved their food.

The women were told that they would be questioned soon. They left for Carolina's apartment. All settled down with iced tea or

water—beverages they had craved during most of
their dinner. They had questions to ask Carolina.

"What about Mike? What did he do?" asked
Annie.

"He set up Larry, the Stripper. That's about the
size of his evil. He was petty, more like an evil
leprechaun than a mass murderer. The rest was
mostly in our imagination," Carolina saying "our"
with lots of guilt. "He will be gone soon, I think,
now that we know what he's like. He's been
pinching too many behinds. And he lied to us,
making up that background he patched together.
The police told me that his father was Swedish.
Mike was passing the delivery truck outside and
did put the bag of cat food back on the truck,
thinking it might be Margie's. It was easy. The
truck door was open and screened him from sight
of the residents. The delivery man was inside
talking to the concierge but had already removed
Margie's bags from the truck to the pavement.
That's why the cat got the poison in the tuna and
not Margie."

"He likes to drink and that's what he goes to do
most nights. He likes to do pranks too," said
Margie, showing her belated astuteness with
people.

"What about Frieda?"

"She's just a woman who likes to talk to men,
dislikes cats and doesn't like Margie. Paula played
on her somehow, like I said. We may find out
more later. She may shut up now when she thinks
about how she was acting—listening to Paula,
saying she'd seen Margie with the masks."

"I had a feeling this situation was more like Iago in *Othello* than Laertes in *Hamlet*," Carolina continued. "Laertes was a straightforward man, involved in a complicated plot at the end to kill Hamlet but was not the evil mind behind it with the poisoned heart; that was the King, who used poisoned swords, poisoned wine. No one was encouraging Iago to kill another like Laertes was being urged to do. Iago was the evil one, pulling the strings, being a fiend, disguised like Paula had disguised herself."

"What connection did the fortune teller have with Paula?" Rita asked Carolina.

"None. There was no person pulling another's strings, like I said. That accusation of being harassed by the fortune teller was Paula's quick thinking to get out of having her fortune told. She believed that Madame Tsarita could really tell fortunes, I guess. It must have been Paula's guilty conscience that made her so afraid."

"Can't she tell fortunes?" Rita asked in a disappointed voice.

"That doesn't mean she can't be right. She's a very perceptive woman. Anyway, we were lucky we threw away containers that might have been tampered with. I wonder what else Paula put the poison in. You were not so wrong, Dot, about temporarily buying toothpaste in metal containers."

"I discarded lots of things like my food and make-up. That was fun," said Rita.

The rest of them thought of all of the other things they should have thrown away and felt queasy. Who would have thought a madwoman was entering their apartments and tampering with their things? Maybe Margie's and Carolina's, since they were always getting into trouble, but not the rest of the group or anyone at all in the whole Courte!

"So it was Paula who tried to push me off the sundeck," Annie said with sudden insight.

"Yes," answered Carolina sadly. "She was the one hiding in the shadows and taking advantage of other likely people being around."

Everyone was very tired. A policeman came to the door saying Paula had confessed to everything she'd done; they had their evidence and would be around the next day to interview them, except for Margie who was needed downtown the next day since she was the victim and might need to be tested for long-term poisoning effects.

Margie suddenly looked like one of the undead.

"Don't worry, Margie, I'll come with you," Carolina assured her.

"We all will, if you want us," the others chimed in.

"You're free for the night," said the policeman again.

""Free?" said Margie. "Me, too?"

"Yes," said the young policeman, confused by the question. He was one who had not been there before nor questioned nor ever arrested Margie. "Have you done something we should know about?"

"No, No, No! Really!"

Carolina stepped in to ask when they should be at the station.

"Someone will call, ma'am. We have your phone numbers." He left.

"Double check your food and drink supplies and then we are free," said Carolina.

"I used to wonder why Paula was here. It was not just that she seemed younger," said Dot. "She didn't seem suited to this place and not to us at the table. She was too perfect and should have been in some penthouse or something."

Annie changed the subject altogether. "I don't think I like Floyd as much anymore. He's too involved with women. I'll listen to him play the piano but don't want his personal attention."

"So Paula was tired of hearing about my ex-husband," said Margie sadly. "I'm sorry I bothered her."

"Forget it. She tried to kill you," said Dot. "And she should have heard you last year!"

Margie cheered up, thinking she was getting better.

"And stop singing those songs in the halls like 'I'd Rather Go Blind' and about seeing your husband run away or something," said Rita. "Or just stop singing in the halls or they *will* take you away."

"Or everyone will try to kill us again if I annoy them too much," giggled Margie, the irrepressible.

CHAPTER 24: CAROLINA'S DREAM

Carolina fell asleep, but soon woke to the sound of the telephone. Margie was hysterical again.

"Is Apolonia sick again?" asked Carolina.

"No, worse."

"Oh, no. Dead?"

"Well, no. She's gone. Gone!"

"I'll be right down."

Carolina threw on a blouse and skirt, remembering to take off her hairnet, her waves and spit curls having been freshly set the night before.

She got to Margie's apartment. The door was open for her as usual. She entered the apartment to find Margie crying.

"Where can she be? She can't get out of the apartment. She used to run out sometimes but became scared by the sound of the elevator or I caught her right away. She wouldn't just leave. She likes this apartment better than the last one."

Carolina had a vision of Apie sneaking out silently past Margie when she opened the door and waiting by the elevator until blind Mr. Maclain went by and then, following him out the outside door. But why? To chase birds, of course. Or to warn that rumored coyote to stay away from the place or his days were numbered. Maybe she wanted to meet the Grand Council of Supreme Cats in the local labyrinth. She'd probably be fighting for more female representation. Or maybe it was time to negotiate with humans for cats' rights.

Back to reality, Carolina, she told herself.

"Could she have been kidnapped?"

"I did find this note." Margie produced it for Carolina.

The note was in block lettering on one of the notepads the Courte gave away once in a while. It said: "APOLONIA IS WITH ME. I'LL CALL YOU"

"Did you get a call, Margie?"

"No, but I was out for a while and didn't see the note right away. I put out food when I went to bed, thinking Apie was under the bed somewhere or just not hungry. I woke in the night to see that she was not on the bed and that her food had not been touched. She isn't here. That's when I found the note."

"She may be here. Let's look again." They searched again, thoroughly.

"She's gone, Margie. Let's search the hallways and public bathrooms and common rooms." They did. No Apie. It was morning by the time they got back.

"Margie, you stay here in case the phone rings. I'll detect."

Carolina left Margie and walked toward her apartment to get her walking stick, but found she had it in her hand and it was turning into an umbrella.

She ran into Ike in the hallway but he was wearing a trench coat.

"What's wrong, Precious?"

"Precious? I'm Carolina, your neighbor."

"Do you need a private Dick? You look screwy," said the man with the yellow-grey eyes.

"Margie's cat, Apolonia, is missing. Someone left this note." She showed him.

His response was, "Have you got a boyfriend? Your boyfriend probably did it. It happened to me too, with a dame. You can't trust nobody. Is a statue missing with the cat? You can hire me to find the facts. Here's my business card. Sam Spade. Don't go hiring that fat detective in 112 either. He's lazy."

Carolina left to go to Apt. 112. She knocked only to hear the voice of a man asking through the door if she had an appointment. The voice said the "great man" never saw a client without an appointment.

"But it's an emergency! Apolonia is missing. We are neighbors, I think, although this looks like the front of a brownstone. Has he retired here?"

"Him? Never. We never age, especially the great Nero Wolfe."

"Please let me talk to him."

"I'll see." The man left but Carolina was lucky. The man with the lovely voice opened the door to reveal an equally handsome man.

"Neighbors deserve special treatment today," he said.

The stout man behind him had come down in his elevator to see his cook about a vital question. Somehow her umbrella had gotten her through the door. She walked up to the heavy man, who recoiled, but she said, "I'm a guest in your house now. Help me find Apolonia. Margie can't stand any more loss!"

"I have to see my chef who seems to be missing too as well as the kitchen. Otherwise, I'd be in my plant room." The stout man seemed to look like Milton who sat near Carolina's table but without Milton's sense of humor. Carolina didn't dare ask where Maxine, his wife, was. She thought asking about his wife might make the man very, very angry.

The handsome young man asked her to sit in a red leather chair and the big man sat at his desk. "My advice to you is let your operatives do the investigating. They'll report to you and the answer is usually simple." The blond man frowned at that. "How are the Phalaenopsis Aphrodite growing in your apartment?"

Carolina noticed that the blond man looked like Floyd, the womanizer, would have looked 60 years ago, except that Floyd was shorter. Floyd, whom the big detective called Archie, showed her out. She found herself standing in front of a normal Courte door. She looked at it in a bewildered way, holding onto the handle of her closed "brolly"—she meant, umbrella. The handsome head popped out again, "Did you try the lawyer on the third floor, Miss Seeton? I heard he may be as good as a detective too. If you need help here, make an appointment. But I don't think the great man will see you now if he thinks you're an hysterical woman." The door closed.

"Me, hysterical? If they think I'm hysterical, I'll send Margie here and see how they cope!"

The elevator got to the third floor, and she walked to the door across from it which opened into an office. How could an office be here? Businesses were forbidden at the Courte. She peeked into the doorway to find a woman at a desk.

"Do you have an appointment?" the woman asked.

"Well no, but Floyd sent me. At least, I think it was Floyd. Did you know there's a brownstone on the first floor?"

"I know Floyd," the woman said with a misty look. "I'll call my boss's secretary to see if the lawyer will see you. It must be an emergency."

"It is!"

The phone was answered and a very pretty woman with brown hair walked out into the reception room. The receptionist called her Della. She was extremely well dressed like Angie, the assistant to the Courte's manager.

Angie heard Carolina's story. "Seeing that you are a neighbor and I love animals, you can come in now and meet Mr. Mason." She obviously had clout.

The two women stepped into an office with a distinguished-looking man sitting behind a large desk. He had the dignity of Mr. Howard, the night concierge. Both were comfortable sitting behind a desk; but the lawyer, of course, had a lot more power and brains.

"Sit down, Miss Pennsbury. I can only give you a few minutes. Do you have the ransom note?"

"Yes, I have the note. No one has called my friend, Mrs. Belbuck, about it."

The man looked at the note.

"How old is the cat?"

"About four, I think."

"What color is the cat?"

"A black and beige calico with white trim."

"Did the cat have any enemies?"

"Well, someone did try to poison her lately."

"I'll have to call in my detective if this is a big case. Can you pay a retainer?"

"I didn't bring my purse."

"You'll have to give me a coin, at least, to make it legal if you want to hire me. It seems to me you can look for the cat yourself. Old ladies who sew, tend to like cats. Maybe someone in a sewing circle would have seen your cat walking by or noticed if someone was carrying a cat. Of course, it could have been clandestinely carried away in a bag."

"I'll get some money and come back, but it's not a court case; nobody's been arrested, although I wish I'd known you were here. My friend Margie keeps getting arrested."

"All of my clients are not guilty, remember," the lawyer said sternly.

"Oh, Margie never is! All arrests with no convictions!"

Carolina got up to leave, not knowing where to go next. The sweet lady said good-bye and showed her out the back way, the traditional way for clients to leave when the police were after them. Then Carolina realized that the police were not after her.

But there was a man with a long, friendly face and a nose like a beak, walking down the hall in dress clothes, using his walking stick like a cricket bat. She thought she saw something move under his top hat and thought maybe she had found Apolonia! She confronted the man.

"Why in heaven's name is a man like you here in the Courte instead of at a Mayfair party?"

"Me? I'm visiting an old friend I knew in the War, don't you know? I can't remember his name so don't ask. We were going to drink some vintage wines and fix his old Daimler. He should be in one of these apartments."

"Give me Apolonia, the cat you have hidden under your hat."

"Lost your cat, have you? No, I haven't seen it. Show you my top hat? Jolly glad to oblige." He showed Carolina the inside of his hat where she saw the initials "L P"—probably for "Lord Peter." She could see the tail of a rabbit moving deep inside the hat.

"I'm sorry to have bothered you," she apologized, thinking he reminded her of her friend, the Captain, although he looked nothing like him. It was something about his polite manner.

"Cheerio!" the elegant man said. "I hope you find the little blighter."

Carolina then found herself in front of the door of Gretchen, the organizer of the sewing circle. She remembered what the lawyer had said about women in sewing circles and cats. Gretchen's door had flowers all over it, fresh flowers and plants reminiscent of an English countryside. She knocked with her umbrella to find Gretchen welcoming her in. The apartment was realistically decorated in pre-war English village style to the last detail.

"Have you heard, Gretchen? Apolonia is gone. We found a note." Carolina showed her the note.

"Sit down, Carolina. I'll get you some tea. I haven't seen your sampler yet," she said, rather accusingly.

"Come to my apartment after we find Apie. I'll be happy to show it to you. I don't want tea. I'm in a hurry. The lawyer upstairs suggested I talk to the sewing circle. Can you call the rest of them to see if they've seen Apie?"

"Stay, Carolina. I do think rushing about like you are is not the best way to investigate." Gretchen looked at her over the top of her glasses. "Who saw her last?"

"Margie did. Last night, she didn't notice the cat was missing until dawn almost."

"Very careless, I think, although the ways of cats are mysterious, unless you know them well.

Apolonia seems to me to be a very sensitive cat. She reminds me of a cat we had when I was a girl. That cat was very artistic. It made lovely paw prints. I'd look into the arts, maybe a museum or art school, if I were you. Or Apolonia may be comforting a friend. Cats are very comforting, you know. Margie reminds me of a neighbor's cousin's mother-in-law I once knew in the Village. Very excitable the woman was. Members of her family would each leave for days to get a rest from her, although she was an admirable, respectable woman—never divorced, of course." The woman with the remark with some censure.

Carolina thanked her, promising to bring Aunt Ida's sampler to the next sewing circle meeting.

"You really should learn to tat, Carolina. It's very calming, unlike crochet—all of that stitch counting. You should send Margie to learn from Carla, although she'd have to sit still or be asked to leave."

Carolina left the cottage where the letter box said "Miss Marple" and found herself in what looked like a corridor in the Courte. She was bewildered and missed the tranquil cottage setting, wishing she'd had the tea she'd been offered there. She was sure it would have been delicious and served with the authentic accompaniments by a faithful maid.

She could think of nothing else to do now but to go back to Margie's apartment to report on her failure and ask which leads they should follow up. She strangely felt like making a sketch of the missing cat, when her umbrella seemed to vanish

as she came to Margie's door. She heard
commotion inside. She tried the door to find it
was open and to find a tableau of four people
around a small but gorgeous calico cat.

Margie, Annie, Dot, Rita and Apolonia all
looked at her as she came into the living room
from the hall.

"What happened while I was gone?" asked
Carolina.

The whole room was lit by sunshine.

Dot answered, "Oh, Annie had her. She'd
gotten hold of the DVD of *Camille* from behind
the concierge desk. You know how they hang
things back there on nails or in wire baskets.
Annie didn't want to watch the movie alone so
came looking for friends. Margie didn't answer,
but her door was unlocked. Annie came in and
saw Apolonia who looked lonely."

Annie interrupted. "Apie let me know that she
wanted to see *Camille* with me. I left Margie a
note so she wouldn't worry. I forgot to sign my
name; you know how things go in these retirement
homes. I was so excited too. Apie and I went to
the game room to watch the movie and I closed
the door. No one noticed us. It was beautiful! Apie
cried a bit too. Who wouldn't?"

Margie said, "Well, maybe Beverly, Frieda,
Ike, Paula, Mike…."

"Stop!"

Annie continued, "I tried to bring her back up
after, but Margie's door was locked. I figured
Margie would call me later. I took Apie back to

my apartment and fell asleep in my chair thinking of Marguerite and Armand—you know, Camille is really Marguerite. I woke in the morning to find Apolonia in my lap. She wanted to come home. She was a bit agitated."

"I waited until I knew Margie would be up and dressed; it isn't polite to visit before a certain time. By that time, Dot and Rita were in Margie's apartment, to be with her. They couldn't find you, Carolina. When I arrived, we all gathered around Apolonia, and then you came in as if by magic. I'm so sorry for not signing my name to the note. I was in a hurry and it seemed like such a good idea to take her. I should have waited. I'm sorry."

Margie, who attracted drama to herself more than Camille ever did, hugged Annie. "It's okay, Annie. I know what it's like to be so excited about something—like seeing a picture of your ex-husband."

Carolina scolded Margie. "You finally took the pictures you had of him down. You're starting a new life, Margie."

Then Carolina sat down, completing the magical circle of friendship. Apie jumped off the table to use the litter box and find some food, her cat side taking back over.

"I'm sure Apolonia enjoyed her vacation very much, but we must be careful about leaving messages and signing our names, although this one gave me a sort of Wonderland adventure mixed with Oz," Carolina said dreamily before her alert self resurfaced.

The others looked at her curiously.

Margie said, "I think Apolonia loves movies. She's very artistic and sensitive."

"So I've recently been told," said Carolina.

They heard the cat loudly munching dry food in the kitchenette area, not sounding too sensitive.

But they all agreed, especially Annie.

"I see we're learning to communicate better so hopefully such a mishap won't happen again..." Carolina found herself still lecturing her friends, as she opened her eyes to see the first light coming into her bedroom. *I have to visit Gretchen soon. I really want to have tea there and would love dinner with Milton and Floyd if they find their cook and.......*

CHAPTER 25: RESOLUTION

Five concerned faces looked at Carolina at dinner.

"Good times have come back. What's wrong?" asked her best friend, Annie.

"Aren't you sleeping, Carolina?" asked Margie.

Before anyone could question her further, Carolina stopped them. "I'm fine. Nothing is wrong. I didn't sleep last night but I enjoyed my dream. We all have to have a reaction to important things that happen to us and my reaction happened last night. As some of my students used to say, 'It was a trip.' Let's welcome the Captain here and put him on the hot seat." She smiled at her friend who'd been temporarily invited to join them as the sixth seat, only a few days after Paula had been carted away. This time he didn't sit at a separate table. The women at the table wished the Captain could be Paula's permanent replacement, however impossible that was.

"Not too hot, I hope," the Captain began by saying. "Paula was a very deranged person, but intellectually brilliant. The Courte can thank you ladies that there weren't more deaths. We had to spend a long time here searching for poisons and other lethal forms for causing homicide."

"Did you find anything?" asked Annie with a bit of unhealthy enthusiasm.

"Let's just say we think it's pretty safe here now."

Margie was too overwhelmed to speak, knowing she'd been the chief target, and didn't like the words 'pretty safe' used together.

"What about the cameras they had in here? Did the police find out anything incriminating about Paula?"

"Not really," continued the Captain. "The investigators mentioned that they saw lots of odd behavior by the residents, but it will forever remain a secret. Paula did hint that she'd been preparing to do something quite bad to Ivan because he apparently noticed something fishy when he walked through Paula's apartment and saw all of her locked doors. He knew something wasn't right about her mailing habits too and she'd begun to hint to him about paying him for his silence. So, being ridden out of town on a rail saved Ivan's life."

"So, visions of blackmail schemes danced in Ivan's head," giggled Margie.

"Yes, I'm afraid Ivan had his own agenda with the cameras," the Captain agreed. "And, as far as what the cameras found, let's just say, at least one of the residents here did not always live up to his marital promises."

"Who? Who?" laughed a delighted Annie, whose own husband would never have strayed from his darling, so she could safely laugh.

Dot, who was wearing one of those odd hats like the Princesses Beatrice and Eugenie had worn to William and Kate's royal wedding, surprised them more by asking, "Does his last name begin with 'M'?"

"I can't say because of professional ethics."

"Oh, my! You asked about Mr. Mealey, Dot! Did you see something he was doing in the hall?" asked Rita.

"No, but his wife is so dismal. That's probably it."

"I guess I was too," murmured an upset Margie who was always ready to blame herself.

"No, Margie, there was no excuse for your husband's dishonest behavior," consoled Carolina. "Everyone knows how some awful people have the nicest spouses. It's complicated, involving upbringing and other factors." She stopped herself from pontificating and tried to change the subject, asking the Captain about other criminal behavior.

"Well, a lot of food is being hidden and transported through the hallways. I'll just tell you again that I couldn't talk about crimes under investigation if I wanted to," he said mysteriously. "No one here is under any serious investigation," he assured some of the worried faces around him who might have taken some hard boiled eggs or lox and bagels to their rooms at some time in the past. The Captain finished his dinner, but declined the invitation to meet together in Carolina's apartment for coffee. He had work to do.

"That was kind of him to meet with us like he did," Rita said. "I wish I could find a man just like him."

"Someone should run an illegal dating bureau from here for lovelorn residents," said Dot rolling her eyes.

But Rita had sounded so wistful that Carolina had felt sorry for her, assuring her, "You have us to support you in whatever you want in life. You see from all this, that we all help each other like a family whenever trouble comes to any of us."

They all got up to go. Carolina held each one's hand as she left, reluctant to let them go. They were so precious to her. But she knew the present danger was gone. This situation had not been one of greed, but of instability. Stability was the norm again, as much of a norm as stability can be. Change was inevitable. Like what was going to happen to that sixth seat at the table that was now available?

THE END

ABOUT THE AUTHOR

 Helen Grochmal was raised in a coal town in Pennsylvania until sent to college by the Great Society of the 1960s. After graduation from what is now Wilkes University, she worked in the Civil Service to pay her way through an M.A. in English from Penn State and an M.L.S. in Library Service from Rutgers. Working as a professional librarian for over 20 years, Helen published various articles in library journals, ending her career as an Associate Professor at a state university in Pennsylvania. She began writing fiction in her 60's when she moved to a retirement home with her cat. In addition to the two books in the Carolina Pennsbury mystery series, she has recently been trying her hand at writing flash fiction and short stories. So far, one piece has been published in *With Painted Words* and another accepted in *Minerva Rising*.

www.ingramcontent.com/pod-product-compliance
Lightning Source LLC
Chambersburg PA
CBHW050423260626
47156CB00003B/1125